To all the elegant ladies out there,
especially my mother.
Thank you.

I dedicate this first book, to my daughter,
Shakara Jade Glassé.

Acknowledgements

First and foremost to my heavenly father,
who has given me the gift of life with many blessings.

To Mum, Dad and Banf.

My sisters, Patsy, Barbara, Paulette, Marcia, Sandy, Deloris,
Carol, Doroth, Sweetie, Joy, and Marcella.

My brothers, James and Ishmal.
My nieces and nephews.

All my friends overseas, especially Helen and Donna.

My co-workers, Cynthia, Olivia, Gretchen, Julett, Ann, Pura,
Yolanda, Jennifer, Terry, Michael, Bill and Cindy.

Special thanks to: Toddra Bunyan, Michelle Hicks-Levy,
Michael Pemberton and Xenia Alvarenga, for being my readers
throughout this whole writing experience.

Thank you to my readers for the prayers and support.

Elegant

Emma Trent

Suzanne A. Glassé

Order this book online at www.trafford.com
or email orders@trafford.com

Most Trafford titles are also available at major online book retailers.

Edited by: G. Jill Todd

Cover artwork/design by: Suzanne A. Glassé

Designed by: Suzanne A. Glassé

Print information available on the last page.

ISBN: 978-1-4251-6987-9 (sc)
ISBN: 978-1-4269-9171-4 (e)

Trafford rev. 07/09/2021

 www.trafford.com

North America & international
toll-free: 844-688-6899 (USA & Canada)
fax: 812 355 4082

One

Every day, rain or shine she sits there, waiting. What is she waiting for, who is she waiting for?

For the past ten years Emma has parked her car in the same designated spot, facing the bench where she sits. It is not possible to miss her. Day after day as Emma pulls up, there she is looking at her, despite the fact they have never exchanged words. Sometimes she'll give a wave and bow her head to the side as though she is shy. More often than not, she has no bags, just a purse she keeps on her lap. She's not the dirty, begging, usual foul-smelling, homeless woman, no, she's tall, sandy brown hair, clear complexion, not sure whether she's black, white or mixed race. She wears tinted glasses and pale colored lipstick, which gives a sheen to her small lips. She always wears her hair pinned up much like a French twist and dresses in high-collared, lace-trimmed blouses. Emma notices each day she wears a different lace blouse, recognizing the different lace patterns on the sleeves and neckline. They are not cheap, neither are the slacks she wears and moccasins. Some days she'll wear a silk shawl thrown over her shoulder.

Office employees love to gossip. Some mornings when in the elevator there was gossip about the woman on the bench. Some said she had millions and her husband stripped her of everything she owned, but then again, maybe she blew it on drugs and rehab programs. There was one who said she had a child and her husband's mistress stole the baby, so he had her committed on the grounds that she was crazy, but despite all this, no one knew anything for sure. Whoever she is or was, she never lost her dignity to carry herself well.

On the days that Emma really notices her, she reminds her of a lady sitting watching the kids playing in the park, or something. Whatever rumors are true or false, she is a beautiful lady. Emma went one step further and thought 'elegant', that's the word, an 'elegant' lady. Emma wondered if she had a family, friends, anyone, or did the bench remind her of a different place and time?

When at home, the lady on the bench does not enter Emma's mind, so she guesses it is true what they say, *'Out of sight, out of mind'.*

Emma is so caught up with work and family ties, thinking about her thirtieth birthday tomorrow, and what to do that's not offensive to Aunt Lou. Oh, you have to meet Aunt Lou, Emma's mother's older sister - beautiful woman, tall, medium frame, golden complexion - you would never believe she was black, *until she opened her mouth sometimes.* She has loose curled hair full of bounce in shades of brown, hazel eyes and a smile that would brighten any room, her laugh is so contagious. She spends a lot of time back and forth from England, so she has a slight, well-spoken British accent. She cares about Emma's well-being, which sometimes Emma thinks twice about, but having no children of her own Emma is her niece and daughter. Emma has no siblings, at least on her mother's side anyway, and her father, well, that's a different story entirely.

Emma often wonders if her mother would be proud of her. She left when Emma was two or three. Everyone has a different time when she left; Aunt Lou doesn't talk about her, Aunt May constantly puts her down and Aunt Gracie, well... Aunt Gracie just stares, you know, she wants to say something, but doesn't. There are no pictures, no letters, no documents on either of Emma's parents; no one seems to know if they're dead or alive. Emma assumes her father is still alive, on account of the fact that Aunt Gracie slipped up one day while they sat around the dinner table having Sunday dinner on Emma's sixteen birthday, fourteen years ago.

"I saw Mint last week; he's now CEO of-"

Aunt Lou interrupted in her passionate voice with that well-spoken British accent.

"Gracie, can you get the bread out of the oven, please, it seems I may have forgotten it?"

Emma knew that was Aunt Gracie's cue to shut up, because the look Aunt Lou gave her was... well, you know. Mint was

3

never mentioned again, but Emma figured he was either her father or had something to do with her and lived in the area, or near, where Aunt Gracie lived. Emma didn't pursue asking any questions about him, she just let it go.

Aunt Gracie lived just under four hours from Aunt Lou, and Aunt May lived two hours away from Aunt Gracie, why so far apart was beyond Emma. Well, maybe my mother took it one step further and left the state all together, Emma thought.

Emma shook herself out of this daydream and walked toward the window. There she was, still sitting there on the bench staring at something in her hand. From a distance Emma could not see what it was, and when she held it close to her heart she just knew it was something special. The windows to the office are tinted and Emma knew the woman couldn't see her, but sometimes she got the feeling she was watching her and that she could see her through them. Emma didn't know why, after ten years, she would be remotely interested in this lady. Yes, she admitted to herself, I admire her and have noticed her attire on many occasions, but I've not even so much as bought her lunch on a rainy day. I say good morning in passing her to and from my car or sometimes just wave, and in the evening I do the same, just a wave, bye. Emma caught herself thinking strongly about the woman on the bench again. What was so special about today?

Emma moved away from the window and walked back

toward her desk, as her assistant knocked on the door, brought her morning coffee and placed it on the desk. As usual, KJ would join Emma and they talked about the soaps from the previous night, mainly taking notice of the different designer gowns the characters wore and comparing notes for their own line of fashion. This had become a ritual for both of them to start the morning right.

Emma made mention of the lady on the bench to her assistant, KJ, quite casually, so she wouldn't get all wound up on her and give her the crazy look.

"Have you ever noticed that lady on the bench, KJ?" Emma asked, ever so subtly.

"What about her?" KJ said nonchalantly.

"Oh, nothing."

Emma was holding the cup of coffee in both hands, staring into space. KJ pulled her chair closer and sat in front of Emma after putting sugar and cream in her coffee. The way she pulled up her chair, slowly, and brushed the top, meant get prepared for a motherly talking to and forget the soaps.

KJ spoke with a ghetto tone, staring into Emma's eyes.

"Okay, I've been your assistant now for ten years, don't you think I know when something is bothering you? Spill whatever it is, now."

Emma responded with agitation, still holding her coffee.

"I don't know."

"Well, why don't you try talking about it, are you still confused about your sexuality, Emm?" KJ said in a low, soft concerned voice, tilting her head to one side looking at Emma.

"*No*, girl," Emma said, sounding black, which she had tried so hard not to do, almost spilling her coffee.

It was not that she was ashamed of who she was, but because Emma loved being Emma; a sophisticated black woman.

KJ paused, looked at the window, pushed the chair back and stood up looking at Emma with attitude.

"Okay then, what?"

Emma looked at the window, sending KJ into a frenzy and causing her to walk toward it.

"I know you don't want to invite that homeless lady to your house and feed her then find out she has fifteen kids, collects welfare and has fifteen baby daddies who work the streets."

KJ did not stop for air; with hands on hips, and swinging her right hand from left to right clicking her fingers, sounding and acting real ghetto (okay... she, I mean, *was!*). Emma looked up at the ceiling.

"God, I know you sent KJ to me for whatever reason and I haven't regretted it since, but, Lord, maybe after this conversation if she doesn't go back to being a refined black woman, I'm going to have to rethink that." Emma thought silently. "It has nothing to do with my sexuality," she said, responding to KJ's question before her ghetto mentality stepped in, surprised KJ would think that of her, knowing her past.

Although she did have a hard time coming to terms with her sexuality, she had finally realized she only liked women as friends and assistants, not partners or lovers. KJ made her come to terms with that when they first met. Emma voiced her sexuality opinion clearly to KJ so there would be no confusion, and the question wouldn't be asked again, however, she didn't think it had really sunk in.

KJ walked back and sat in the chair across from Emma, leaned back in the chair looking at her, shaking her head.

"Then what is it? I know you're thirty tomorrow, and Emma, I would love to be you right now!" KJ paused, followed by a sigh then she quietly described Emma's features and position. "Tall, medium frame, honey complexion looking like a doll, long wavy hair almost naturally blonde, green eyes, a beautiful smile, educated with a Bachelors and a Masters all before your twenty-first birthday. Vice president of this wonderful design company and single, what could you possible be thinking about? Your mom, Ms. Lou, I hope she ain't sick, is she?"

"KJ, "Emma said, irritated by her incorrect grammar. "It's *isn't* sick, and no, she's fine." Emma paused for a second then whispered, "I never mentioned this before, but, Lou is my aunt,

7

not my mother."

Holding her head down, Emma felt a little embarrassed keeping that away from KJ, knowing they have grown so close over the years. KJ walked around to Emma's side of the desk and reached to hug her from behind the chair, instead she gave her a kiss on the top of her head.

"Is that what's bothering you, you felt you needed to be open with me about Lou? Don't let that worry your pretty little head, I forgive you." Before going back to the other side of the desk, KJ patted Emma's shoulder twice and continued speaking whilst walking toward the door. "Let's get back to work, Emm, we have deadlines to meet, we'll talk about your real mom another time, when you're good and ready."

Closing the door behind her, KJ left the office, leaving Emma still perplexed. Emma, still confused as to why she was feeling that way, needed to know what KJ felt about the woman, or she wouldn't rest for the day, so she called KJ back to her office and asked her to take a seat.

"If you're firing me, Emma Trent-" KJ said, before she sat down, waving her hands and acting ghettoish and defensive, but, before she could go any further with the drama, Emma stopped her.

"Wow, what happened to *Emm*? Using my entire name... and no, I'm not firing you," Emma said, getting the record straight before continuing. "I just want to know how you feel about something or someone."

The smile returned to KJ's heart-shaped face. Sometimes she could be so defensive from out of the blue, and Emma could never figure her out. KJ was of medium height, small framed, chocolate complexion, dark brown eyes and shoulder length hair cut into a bob. When Emma first met KJ (real name Karen Jenkins) she was working the streets trying to make a living, and Emma was her first stop. She never had to make another one since. She needed money and Emma needed to know who she was. Now she made money and Emma knew who she was.

KJ and Emma never really talked about how they met to anyone. They joked about it together sometimes, but that was it. Emma told KJ her dream of becoming the CEO of a great design firm; they both laughed, thinking it impossible. Now, ten years on, Emma was vice president and KJ was her assistant. KJ no longer had that very low self-esteem and lack of confidence in her reading ability, like she did when she first met Emma. She was going to university part time, working on her Bachelors in business administration. Although fifteen years Emma's senior, KJ was like the big sister Emma never had.

KJ meant a lot to Emma. The thing she loved most about her was her frankness and honesty; if KJ thought it, she voiced it, and sometimes she made Emma feel bad in a good way, if that's possible. Maybe it was because she saw the truth for what it was.

"What do you want to know about the lady on the bench, Emm?" KJ asked in a concerned voice, knitting her eyebrows together.

Emma sat up in her chair, put her hands behind her head, tilted her head back as though to relive a stretch then put her hands on the desk and leaned forward.

"You called her a lady, not woman, not homeless, but lady," Emma said, confusing KJ. "You called her a lady, why?" Emma repeated, staring into KJ's face.

"Lady, woman, what's the difference? She's a homeless female," KJ responded.

"No, KJ, when you call someone a lady it means they show a high degree of respect for themselves, they carry themselves differently from a woman, they hold their head up high, people admire them. Ladies have people working for them, they don't work for people, they have a place in society."

Emma could feel herself getting all caught up, and the lost look on KJ's face made her stop. She sat back in her chair and closed her eyes for a split second when she noticed KJ looking at her in a funny way, turning her head slightly, but watching her at the same time.

"Would you like a glass of water?" KJ stuttered.

"No thank you," Emma replied, feeling somewhat

embarrassed.

KJ stood up and walked toward the window in Emma's office; she looked out and saw the woman on the bench.

"From a distance she sure is beautiful," she said, still looking out of the window. "I wonder what brought her to this?" KJ stared as though in a trance as she continued. "Emm, do you remember your first job?"

As Emma was about to answer, KJ put her hand up.

"Let me continue, please." Still looking through the window staring at the woman, KJ continued. "When we met you were a twenty-year-old graduate, confused about your sexuality. You were working at Ms. Rose's boutique or starting here at MB's, I can't remember which, but do you remember?"

KJ turned to look at Emma.

"Yes, I do," Emma said gently, wondering where the conversation was leading.

"While you were in college getting an education, I was being a mother trying to make ends meet with five kids. I was thirty-five years old the day you walked into my life and changed it. My mother walked out on my sisters and me when I was twelve years old, she never looked back. My oldest daughter was twenty-two years old that night we met, do the math and you'll see I had her at thirteen years of age; she's now thirty-two. I was ten when my father first had sex with me... and I mean full-blown sex. He told me in order to become a woman I had to first know how to please a man… I couldn't tell anyone. I had three other sisters, each of us a year apart, and I knew he was doing the same thing to them, although they never said. My two oldest daughters are fathered by my father, and my three other children by his brothers, yes, my uncles, each a year apart."

KJ hung her head and paused for a second, afraid to look at Emma.

"I was banged up… pardon my expression, for five years of my life, back to back, because I had to learn to be a woman, or what I was told a woman had to be. I had to know how to treat the men in my house, before I could have a man outside." KJ looked up at Emma and her tone changed, looking at her as if she thought she was better than she was. "I know you're probably saying to yourself why didn't I leave, run away or something? Well, before you ask, let me answer." KJ walked away from the window toward Emma then stopped. Emma could tell it was painful for her, and in ten years she had never seen KJ like this, she was always so bubbly. Yes, they talked, but never like this. Emma begged her to stop, but she insisted on continuing.

"I've waited for the right moment to talk, all my life, Emm, I've been told to keep quiet every time, please… let me speak."

Emma felt somewhat uncomfortable with KJ like this, but she was prepared to hear her out, hiding her apprehension inside.

"My mother, from what I remember of her, was a stunning woman, always worked and provided food for us. My father stayed home most of the time, getting fired from every job he ever had. He drank a lot too. When he was home in the daytime he was always locked up in the room with a neighbor's daughter or one of my siblings. It didn't bother me at the time, as I wasn't interested in what they were doing, but now I know. My mother came home from work early one day; her cycle had come on she said, and she had messed up her clothes. I didn't know what she was talking about, so I just laughed, but from the look she gave me out the corner of her eye I knew I should not be laughing. She went into the house and up to her room, and found my dad in a compromising position with our neighbor's ten-year-old daughter and my older sister. I will never forget the look on her face, which was the last time I saw my mother and the last time she saw me as a child.

Later that year I found out I was pregnant. My father took me out of school and sent me to live with his brothers in the lower part of town, 'The Hood', until the baby was born. He would visit often, mostly for sex. The following year I had another. When my father could no longer pay my uncles money for my board, I had to pay by sleeping with each of them - there were four. I don't really know who the fathers are for my last three kids, but... I know they belong to my uncles. I was never allowed to leave the house. The neighbor was a midwife and they paid her substantially to deliver the babies and keep quiet."

KJ turned to the blank wall and laughed, tilting her head back, wiping the tears from her eyes. She turned back toward the window and put both hands on the pane as though feeling the glass, but instead she placed her forehead on the glass between her hands and pressed hard then she raised her head and hit it back and forth twice. Emma froze in her seat. She couldn't move, as though something was holding her back. KJ stopped then walked to another part of the window as if trying to look at something. She sniffed and wiped her nose with the back of her hand then onto her skirt, as if going back to childhood stage. Emma reached for the tissues on the corner of her desk. KJ chuckled, and then continued to talk.

"My youngest, Josh, would be twenty-eight years old today; Myron would be twenty-nine and Hew thirty, had they lived."

Emma was stunned by what KJ had just said, and sat farther back in her chair, folding her arms and listening, almost afraid to tell her to stop.

"Enough! KJ, let's get back to work," Emma said at last, fixing the papers on her desk.

"This particular Sunday afternoon," KJ still persistent, continued, "was so bright, all the kids were laughing, having fun playing in the yard, and it was almost a perfect day, until my father decided to show up and insisted on taking the kids for ice cream. I looked at him with a bad taste in my mouth." KJ sounded like she was reliving the moment, expressing the emotions on her face. "Don't look at me like that" she said, deepening her voice, trying to sound like her father. "Can't I take my own grandkids for ice cream? Come on, Karen, I've changed, I've turned my life around." KJ once more used her own voice. "I just looked at the boys as I usually would... cold... and told them to go wash their hands and go with their granddaddy. I couldn't help but mumble under my breath repeating his words, '*turned his life around*.'" Her father's voice spoke again. "What about the girls? I said, he'd better walk with those boys and leave my girls alone. Huh, huh," KJ chuckled. "From the tone of my voice, he realized he should leave while he had the chance and good sense. I would never let my girls go with him, although they were his biological daughters.

The boys left with him around two o'clock to get ice cream, which was literally a ten-minute walk, but my father, as always, wanted things his way and drove his prized, vintage, blue and white Thunderbird car, which he usually took for a spin Sunday afternoons if the weather was good. I remember my youngest, Josh, running up to me to give me a hug. I brushed him away and said, 'go with your granddaddy before he changes his mind'. He looked at me and smiled. I hated them, all three of them."

Emma could hear the anger in KJ's voice.

"They were mine, but I hated them. Every time I looked at them I could see my uncles looking back at me, I could barely touch them."

She wiped her nose again, this time walking toward Emma's desk and reaching for the tissue box. She looked at Emma, her eyes red from the tears, as she picked up the box and walked back toward the window. KJ continued to talk.

"My father was always showing off with the speed that old car had." She paused. Her voice softened. "He was speeding and took a sharp turn, he lost control of the car, he crashed into one of the gas pumps at the corner gas station, the car ignited and they all died on impact. You could see the smoke for miles - they never made it to the ice cream parlor. I was doing my second daughter, Shelly's, hair at the time, when one of the neighbor's kids came running in and said, 'He crashed the car, he crashed the car!' 'I heard you the first time', I said with no motion or emotion, I just continued doing my daughter's hair. I remember looking up at that point and asking if he was dead. The child looked at me and said, 'I think so'. I smiled, and at that point I knew I was free, or so I thought. I was twenty-seven years old and had to make funeral arrangements for my three young boys, all under the age of fifteen.

I was still living with my uncle, his wife and their three kids, with my two daughters. The other three uncles lived close by in the neighborhood. When the police came to the house to confirm the accident and the death of my three boys and father, I stood tall as if I'd just won a battle. The welfare department also came with the police, which was routine when it concerned children. The first question she asked me was if I lived with the father of the children. I looked at my uncle, the welfare officer looked at me then over at him and asked the question again, but this time she asked if I needed to talk to someone she was available. My uncle's wife came over to me and slapped my face then spat at me, pointing in my face, screaming and crying, 'If you ever accuse my husband of being the father of your children after all that he has done for you and your kids, I'll kill you'. She paused for a few seconds in front of me, before walking back to stand side by side with her husband. I will never forget the evil look in her eyes, her trembling mouth, wet from the tears.

The officer asked the question again; that time I had no response and I did not look in my uncle's direction. The policeman never asked any questions, he just looked at my uncle, raised his eyebrows and said, 'Have a nice day, sir'. The welfare officer gave me a tissue, took my arm and escorted me outside the house. We walked toward the broken-down car parked in the driveway, which my uncle had promised to fix and teach me how to drive, but never did. As we walked, the welfare officer asked me a few questions and I answered them explicitly. I could tell from her expression she was disgusted, but I'm not sure who with, it was hard to tell. She asked why I stayed. I looked at her and smiled, I looked down to the ground and shook my head, raised it again and looked straight into her eyes and said, 'If your brother brought home a twenty-seven-year-old woman with five kids, can't read or write, my girls are fathered by my father and my boys to my uncles, what would you do?' She looked at me. I could see the tears welling up in her eyes, she couldn't answer. I looked at her and said, 'What man wants a woman like me?'. She gave me a hug and whispered in my ear, 'Things will get better; you have to believe that, stay strong. I'll do what I can within my power to see to that'.

The state paid for the funeral of my boys, and my mother, after all those years, paid for the funeral of my father. She never attended. My sisters never came or acknowledged his death. I never heard from the welfare officer again until I had to contact her on a different matter. I guess arranging for the state to pay for my boys' funerals was all she could do with the power she had."

KJ had a blank stare.

"The youngest of the four uncles inherited some money from my father's death, they say that he had a hefty life insurance and left Uncle Cliff as his beneficiary. When all was lucid with the courts he received the money. He bought a new house, a car and took his family on vacation, skiing. *Now, where you hear black folks skiing?'* KJ said in a comedic-style voice with hand on hip, leaning to one side. She then laughed, shook her head and grunted. "Hmm..." She paused for a moment then continued.

"When they returned from their skiing trip, I went to see him; that would be our first conversation since he moved out of the house before the accident. I was bold and didn't sugar coat what I wanted, I just asked him for some help, financially. I told him I wanted to buy a house. There was a house for sale three blocks away, very affordable, I'd get a job and support my girls and maintain my house. He looked me up and down, came close to my face as if to kiss me then put his cheek against mine and whispered in my ear, 'I owe you nothing, now get off my doorstep'. I stepped back, barely getting my foot out of the doorway before the door was slammed in my face. I could see him looking at me through the window as I stood there for a few seconds, and then I ran home with embarrassment.

The hurt inside was indescribable. I couldn't sleep for days. I kept having nightmares, waking up thinking he was in my room and seeing the door being shut in my face. I knew I had to do something. A month had passed since I asked for his help. My oldest daughter, Skye, would bring me books to teach myself to read, she also invested in a tape recorder and checked out tapes and books from the library for me to read, listen and learn. I was a fast learner when I put my mind to it.

One day I got up and went to the library - *me*! I taught myself a few things, because it was time for me to help myself. I contacted the welfare officer whom I had not heard from since the day of the accident. When she heard my voice she began with, 'I was meaning to call you, but...' I stopped her right there, I had a few choice words for her in my mind, but I just asked if she still had the papers for me. I know I needed to work on my tone, but... 'What papers?' she asked, all proper and professional. 'You know,' I said, sounding real ghetto, getting irritated. Not being very smart, I wasn't sure what the papers were called or really what to ask for. 'Why don't you tell me what it is you want me to do, and then maybe we can locate what papers you're talking about?' She said it like... I didn't know what I was talking about, which I didn't, but that's neither here nor there.

'Okay,' I said, all embarrassed, knowing I could have handled it differently. I don't know why I was so upset with her, but she helped me. She went over some of the things we talked about that day, and when she touched on sexual harassment I said, 'Yes, that's it'. I couldn't remember the name she had used, but when she said it, oh, I remembered. I asked her if we could proceed with the case against my three uncles for sexual harassment, or was it too late. 'It's never too late for rape charges,' she responded.

'Rape,' I repeated, 'no one said nothing bout no rape, they didn't hold me down or beat me, they were teaching me to be a woman, isn't that right?' I did it again, being loud and aggressive. 'No, Karen, it's rape when an adult is having sex with a child whether the child resists or not, it's rape.' She explained that I was not the only child who went, or was still going through, this, there are thousands of kids today whose parents and family members are using them for sexual pleasures. She also explained the possible consequences I could face if there was no proof to substantiate the facts of rape, 'now being an adult and all the boys are dead and your father too, with regard to your daughters, there is that possibility'. I was willing to take that chance. I thanked her for her time. She asked me to call her within two weeks and she would have some news for me whether good or bad. I hung up the phone with a good feeling about this.

I called her back in two weeks as she had asked. She started with, 'I have good news and bad'. She sounded all excited for someone with bad news. 'Okay, tell me the good news.' My good spirit was gone. 'Well, the courts were able to prove all three uncles guilty of rape of a minor under the age of sixteen and fathering your three boys while you were still under the age of eighteen. They were each sentenced to thirty years in prison, ten years for each of your sons. They will be picked up today from

21

their respective places of employment or residence...'

I didn't know whether to be happy or sad. 'I hope that's the bad news,' I said as she paused. 'No, the bad news is, you were not awarded the money we hoped for. I want you to know, Karen, that you will face them again after ten years. I'm sorry, Karen,' she said. I was praying for a better outcome, but I thanked her for all she had done. That was the last time I heard her voice, or needed to contact her.

Cliff died in prison, they said he had a heart attack; Jim, the one I spent most of my life with, had a stroke and is now wheelchair bound living in the same house. Sometimes I'd walk by and see him sitting in his chair by the window, don't know if he recognized me, don't much care either. Joe, after being released from prison earlier this year, vanished.

When Uncle Jim married Carmel, not being able to read and all, she presented me with some papers and told me to sign, which I did. I did not know they were papers giving up my parental rights of my boys and giving her full custody. At the time I was signing she told me my kids and I would have a roof over our heads as long as we wanted, free of charge. I was grateful to her, until I found out years later that she used me and the boys to claim income tax and welfare. No wonder she never worked!

For seven years I braided hair for the neighborhood kids and babysat for an income, although at that time I was able to read and write, a little slow, but... I lacked confidence. My self-esteem was so low I thought that was all I was good at. I'd look at magazines and duplicate the new styles in the kids' hair, especially for the first day of school. It was like Christmas had came early for me; every parent in the neighborhood brought their girls and boys to have their hair braided - those were some good times. One night I sat on the steps outside the house and a voice said to me, 'Go see Ma Bell'. 'Ma Bell,' I said 'is you crazy? That woman runs a whore house'. The people next door looked at me, laughing, like I was crazy talking to myself. The voice would come back again, 'Go see Ma Bell'. I couldn't take it anymore, so I went to Ma Bell's house. She cleaned me up with fresh clothes and told me how much she expected me to bring back from a night's work. She gave me an address for my first assignment; she sent me to you at Harry's Motel. I will never forget the look on your face. I wasn't going there for sex, I had other motives.

I fell to the lowest of the low to go to Ma Bell's, but I'm so glad I did. I can honestly say I tried to keep myself decent for my girls, despite the heartache, Emm, I tried to stay decent."

KJ was crying uncontrollably and knelt on the floor. Emma walked over to her and held her close. She repeated over and over:

"I tried, Emm, I tried."

"It's over now, that part of your life is over," was all Emma could say to try to convince her, but she still sobbed

"You don't understand."

Emma put her head on KJ's shoulder.

"I know, I don't understand, but what I do know is, Karen Jenkins is now KJ with a new life, a new personality, you can read, write, you passed your GED first time, your AA within two years and now you're working on your Bachelors. You have two wonderful daughters, both successful teachers because you pushed them so hard, and both have the utmost respect for you," Emma said, reminding her of what she had achieved. "You have a fabulous condo fully paid for because you feared losing it. KJ, you are a model for other women out there, including me."

Emma tried to make KJ forget the past and look forward to moving on. KJ hugged her, looking at her with red eyes.

"Thank you for listening, I've just lifted all the weight that's been holding me down all these years."

She stood up from the floor, wiped her eyes, fixed her skirt and smiled at Emma, still crouched on the floor, as she walked toward the door. She closed it quietly as she left Emma's office. Emma watched KJ walk out of her office a different person. She got up from the floor, looked out of the window and tried to figure out what had just happened. She stared at the lady on the bench, and wondered what kind of life did she have or walk away from.

*

KJ avoided Emma for the rest of the day. She brought her afternoon tea to the office as usual, but she didn't join her as she normally would. She smiled and walked out of the office. Emma didn't entertain the way KJ felt for the rest of the day; she gave her that respect.

The afternoon meeting to endorse the new line of garments for the upcoming photo shoot, was always a favorite of KJ's, but when Emma got ready to leave, KJ was not at her desk. Emma was running late, so she couldn't wait for her to return. She left a note on her desk to meet her at the meeting on the third floor. Emma was introducing a new line of clothing on which she and KJ were working. She wasn't sure how Mr. Brown was going to acknowledge the new line, but she was prepared to take a chance and wait for feedback from him, although in the ten years Emma had worked for MB Design, she had never met the infamous Mr. Brown, on the other hand she thought it was a good thing. Maybe if they met, he might have disagreed with some of the cover choices she made and centerfolds for the various magazines over the years. Well, as long as she was promoting fashion and MB Design kept being voted best design company in the world, she didn't think Mr. Brown would have a problem with that.

Emma had a problem with the name, MB Design Company.

With the garments she designed and advertised, and the magazines they promoted, she thought the name should be sensational.

Two

It was six o'clock, and the photo shoot was well under way, considering it had started rather late. Emma kept looking at the entrance door hoping KJ would walk in at any moment, but she never did.

The production crew wrapped up at around nine o'clock that evening. Emma was exhausted. Greg and Naomi, both senior partners, and Emma took the elevator back to the ninth floor to gather their belongings before calling it a night. Emma had to put all the sample fabrics away and Greg had the roll of blueprints for the different runway set ups they would be using for the upcoming events. Naomi supervised and timed each session to make sure they were on schedule.

Being in the design industry was hard work; proofing fabrics, from silk, cotton, polyester, rayon, raw silk to backdrops; color, texture, styles, indoor, outdoor to interviewing models; tall, short, black, white, Asian, African to placing them in categories; hands, feet, hair and eyes. Then there were the magazines, everyone wanted a say in the magazines. It certainly was hard work, not to mention travel - they did that too.

"Hurry up, Greg, I'm just putting these samples on my desk, I'll sort them out in the morning," Emma said as they exited the elevator, going to their respective offices.

"Okay, wait for me; I need to use the john," Greg said, laughing.

"That's too much information, Greg," said Emma, laughing back and almost dropping her samples.

As she approached the double glass doors leading to her office, she was hoping KJ would be there sitting at her desk, working on some project and feeling embarrassed about earlier, but she was wrong. KJ's desk was neat, as always, she never left anything out, she even locked away Emma's message pad, which she had done for ten years. KJ had a thing about trusting people.

"Emma, you ready, girl?" Greg asked, standing outside the glass doors waving, pointing to his watch.

"What, you have a hot date, Greg? Let me rephrase that... hold on, I'm coming," Emma said, picking up her bag, turning out the lights and heading for the open glass doors.

Emma grabbed hold of Greg's arm. She laughed like a schoolgirl as they walked toward the elevator.

Greg was tall, dark, handsome and masculine, on account that he never left the gym. He used to wear braids when they first met, but now he sported that clean bald cut. He had a mustache on his upper lip, those smooth full lips, dark brown eyes and that baritone voice - mm, that voice. He definitely turned the female heads, and he knew it too. He had modeled for a few of MB's magazines some years ago, before Emma's time, until he started working for the company some twenty years ago. Greg must be pushing fifty, and didn't look a day over forty, handsome as hell. As they approached the elevator, Greg asked where KJ was. Emma raised her eyebrows and shrugged her shoulders. He looked at her and smiled, putting his hand in front of her, escorting her into the elevator. The ride seemed ever so long going down, neither of them said anything, she avoided the question. When they got to the ground floor Greg asked where she was parked, and before she could answer he spoke sarcastically, putting his hand over his mouth.

"Oh... I forgot, you're vice president material now."

"Greg, I thought you were over that," Emma said sadly, old feelings stirring up inside.

She stood there in the lobby looking at him, going back to when they had first met ten years before. Emma was introduced to MB Design Company by her former manager, Ms. Rose; she worked for her fresh out of college. It was funny how Emma was hired for the job. She was looking for a white lace blouse and happened to walk into Ms. Rose's boutique.

"Are you looking for work?" the little old lady asked her, just like that.

"Yes," Emma replied, but thought she needed to get back to work.

"What are your qualifications?" she asked.

Emma told her; a Bachelors and Masters in fashion and business administration.

"You're pretty, you look like someone I used to know. I hope you have a good head on your shoulders like she did."

Emma kept looking around, fearing the woman's manager would come out at any given moment. After she questioned Emma further, she introduced herself as Ms. Rose, the sole owner of the boutique, throwing both her hands in the air, praising the Lord. Emma looked around out of the corner of her eye, trying not to offend her, still looking for her boss, but no one else showed up; needless to say she started work the very next day.

Dressed in a beige silk blouse and tailored brown pants suit with beige flat shoes, Emma showed up for work bright and early. Ms. Rose was already there sitting by the counter looking at a small blue book.

"Oh, I'm so glad you came," she said as Emma entered through the doorway.

Why wouldn't I come? Emma thought, but didn't say anything.

"Well, young adults these days think boutiques such as this don't pay well because they don't see a high volume of people coming in and out," Ms. Rose continued. "Come here, Miss

Emm, don't mind me calling you Miss Emm do you?"

"No, not at all."

"Well, good. I want you to know a few secrets to becoming successful." She moved from the counter and started walking around the boutique, still talking. "You see, success is all around you, but you cannot always see it with the naked eye. It's what you *can't* see that makes you wealthy, let me explain. Come sit... I'm sorry, Sugar, did you want some tea or coffee before we get started?"

"I'll have a cup of tea if you don't mind," Emma answered politely.

"Follow me, let me show you where you can make your tea, or coffee if you change your mind."

Emma followed Ms. Rose to a door at the rear of the boutique. The door had an oblong window covered with a floral curtain, and as she pushed it open, Emma was quite surprised. The room had a custom-built unit with a two-stove burner, microwave and toaster on one side, and on the other, a mini dishwasher, sink and a small pantry. In one corner of the room she had a small round table with two chairs and a big, overstuffed, comfy deep pink couch, which unfolded to a single bed.

"Wow, this is so cozy!" Emma said, with her eyes wide open looking around and finding something different in every corner of the room, noticing the pale pink color carpet.

"You must establish a piece of you no matter where you go," said Ms. Rose. "Make your tea and meet me back in the front, Sugar," she said in such a sweet voice, with a smile.

"Okay," Emma responded, watching Ms. Rose walk out of the room closing the door behind her.

Emma continued to look around while waiting for the water to boil. She opened another door that led to the bathroom; there was one surprise after another. The bathroom had a full-size tub, shower, sink and commode, with walls painted a soft pale pink, with pink floral accessories, and she even had pink toilet paper and hand towels. Emma could hear the water boiling and walked back toward the stove. There were three canisters on the counter; one each for tea, coffee and sugar. Emma made her tea and went to meet Ms. Rose in the front. As Emma opened the door, the old lady was sitting at the counter waiting for her.

"Hope you liked what you saw back there?" Ms. Rose said as Emma was approaching her.

"Yes, I did... very elegant," Emma said, hoping she wasn't being too nosy.

"Come and sit here with your tea, you can rest the cup on the counter."

Ms. Rose pointed to a stool she had next to her.

"Thank you," Emma said, moving the stool to make herself

comfortable.

"When you live to see my age," Ms. Rose began, "you get wiser, smarter and wealthier. Notice what I said... *wealthier* not richer, there's a difference." She paused for a moment and looked at the little blue book on the counter in front of her. "Rich people show off what they have," she started again, narrowing her eyes for a split second. "They buy expensive jewelry, cars, houses, have elaborate parties, and most are generally born into it and don't know what to do with it, so they spend because they have it to spend. Wealth is acquired, it's earned and not seen."

"What do you mean *not seen*? You can tell wealth when you see it," Emma said, stating a point, or was she?

"Tell me... what does wealth look like?"

"I'm not sure," Emma said, knitting her eyebrows, putting her forefinger into her mouth.

"You just said you can tell wealth when you see it," Ms. Rose challenged her.

"Maybe I'm confused with riches," Emma admitted.

"When you came into this boutique yesterday, you asked me for a lace blouse, I showed you the various kinds of lace blouses we had. When I approached you to talk to you, you kept looking around, maybe for a manager or boss, stop me if I'm mistaken."

"No, you're not mistaken," Emma answered, feeling ashamed.

"What you saw was a little black woman standing in a boutique, her hands behind her back, waiting for customers to come in, was that what you saw?" she asked, looking at Emma with wise eyes.

"Yes."

Emma held her head down with embarrassment wondering how she had known that.

"What you didn't see was... wealth." She said the word 'wealth' so silently. "You cannot see wealth because often times it's not shown. Because I chose to take the bus, doesn't mean I don't have or own a car, because I chose to dress comfortably to put in a full day's work, doesn't mean I don't have or own elegant attire, so you see, my dear, wealth is a whole new life, wealth requires giving back."

"What do you mean *giving back*?" Emma said naïvely.

"Give back to those who made you successful, no matter whom they are. This little blue book," she lifted the book from the counter, "has a million stories to its name and over forty-five years of loyal clients... Have you finished your tea?"

"Yes, thank you," Emma said, not expecting that question.

"Come with me, Miss. Emm, you can leave the cup on the counter, let me show you something."

Emma followed Ms. Rose to another door at the back of the boutique; this one had a curtain covering the entrance and a heavy padlock near the handle. She pulled a small key from the bunch of keys she had on a spiral rubber key chain around her wrist then opened the door and reached for the light switch to the right on the wall. When she turned the light on all Emma could see were rows and rows of fabric, sewing machines, every color thread, zips, the works.

"This looks like a factory," Emma said, amazed.

"Very close, my dear, but not a factory, this is where it all began - my door to wealth. A few years ago I had an assistant who single handedly made this boutique the success it is today, you remind me of her a lot." Ms. Rose stood there in silence, just looking, she smiled, turned to face Emma and whispered, "Wealth entails hard work."

She walked out of the room and Emma followed her.

"Customers may not come here very often, but they buy every day, what you don't see in front of you, is the silent partner behind you. Remember, wealth is never seen." Ms. Rose walked over to the counter and put the blue book in a small drawer. "Miss Emm, not every day will be a good day, but make every day *your* day. Don't summarize, blame or point the finger for your mistakes, just accept them and move on. When you're misunderstood, someone missed your point. Show who you are by the way you dress, walk, talk and hold a conversation. Never be intimidated; it shows lack of confidence. If your boss strikes out at you with harsh tones or words, don't shed a tear; it's a sign of weakness and you'd have failed the challenge. Are you keeping up with me, Sugar, or would you like me to stop?"

"Um, with all respect, Ms. Rose, I don't know why you're telling me all this, it's very interesting, don't get me wrong, but…" Emma said, eagerly wanting to get to work.

"You may not understand today, why this wise woman chose you, but my intuition and mission, but most of all, my faith, have never failed me yet. The young lady of whom you remind me so much, worked for me many years ago and is the owner of her own empire today." Ms. Rose paused. "When God plants a seed, water it a little every day and before you know it, it'll start to sprout. When you see those shoots, you know the roots are setting in, as the root gets stronger, so does the shoot, before you know it, it has blossomed, but you only planted one seed. When you look to your left there's another shoot, then to your right, another… That's the root, that's wealth spreading, you can't see it, but you're reaping from it." Ms. Rose stopped talking for a moment then continued. "Let me teach you the business."

Thank God, at last I'll get to fix this place up and make it more inviting, Emma thought.

"Where would you like me to start to brighten up this place, Ms. Rose?" Emma asked, excited and eager to get to work.

"Brighten up this place," Ms. Rose repeated, putting her

hands on her hips, tilting her head back and laughing.

"What's so funny? I thought that's what sales assistants do?" Emma said, wondering what could possibly be so amusing.

"A sales assistant," Ms. Rose said quietly, "have you been listening to anything I just said, Miss. Emm?"

"I listened, but I'm not sure that I fully understand."

"Let me repeat. Wealth comes not from those you see, but those you cannot. Don't ever forget that. Just because you make a place fancy, doesn't mean people will buy." Ms. Rose gave Emma a wise old look, and then proceeded. "I'm afraid I've talked you into mid-morning. Would you like another cup of tea before we get started?"

"No thank you," Emma said, wondering if she had made the right decision.

"Okay, let me lock the entrance door. We're going to be working in the back today; I want to familiarize you with different types of fabric, colors, texture, weight, thread and stitching etc."

Emma knitted her eyebrows.

"Why do I need to know all that?"

"Because, Sugar," Ms. Rose said in her quiet voice, "when customers call to place an order for a custom-made gown for a wedding or special occasion, I want you to understand exactly what they are talking about, so you can communicate intelligently to the highly professional seamstresses."

Ms. Rose spoke so softly, but got right to the point. She had a way of looking at you and raising her left eyebrow, suggesting, you do understand don't you? Ms. Rose had a petite frame, was of medium height, with mocha skin and a soft spoken voice, shoulder-length, dark wavy hair and brown eyes. She was very shapely for her age, humble and extremely knowledgeable about fashion - she knew her stuff. To look at her you'd think she was a retired saleswoman working to make ends meet, but she was far from that.

What a day, Emma thought.

*

"Good evening, Emma, I didn't hear you come in," said Aunt Lou. "How was your first day?"

"I'm not sure. I'll tell you when I've rested these feet for an hour."

"Like that was it?" Aunt Lou said, smiling. "It's called work, you'll get used to it."

After soaking her feet, Emma went downstairs and met her Aunt Lou in the sitting room.

"Better?" Aunt Lou asked.

"Much," Emma replied.

Emma struck up a conversation with her aunt explaining some of the things Ms. Rose had talked about, without mentioning her name, but when she told Aunt Lou where she was working, she gave her a bizarre look.

"Why are you looking at me like that?"

"Like what?" Aunt Lou said as though nothing had just happened.

"Never mind," Emma said, brushing it off. "Do you know Ms. Rose, Aunt Lou?"

"Vaguely. I remember buying a few items from her boutique many years ago," Aunt Lou replied, holding a drink in her hand as usual.

"Yes, she has some items that go way back, but she has the best selection of lace blouses."

Aunt Lou looked stunned to hear Emma say that.

"What do you know about lace blouses?"

"That's how I got the job," said Emma. "I went in there looking for a particular lace blouse I saw in the window a few weeks ago. As I was seeking employment, I decided to buy it. When I went in there, she showed me a wonderful range of lace blouses. I think they're so elegant, so I bought three. She started asking me particulars about myself then offered me the position and I accepted."

"All the same?" Aunt Lou said, jokingly.

"All the same, what?" Emma asked, losing track of the conversation.

"All the same blouses," Aunt Lou said, narrowing her brows.

"No, silly, three different kinds," said Emma.

"She's a wise woman, Emma, a very wise woman," Aunt Lou said, rubbing her forefinger around the rim of the glass.

"I thought you didn't know her," Emma said, giving her aunt a strange look.

"I don't. I've heard a lot of people say good things about her, and she's helped many along the way too. She's designed endless wedding gowns, and she..."

Aunt Lou stopped and asked Emma to pour her another drink.

"She what?"

"Oh, nothing... she's a good woman."

Emma could tell by the look on Aunt Lou's face that there was more.

Ms. Rose inherited a large sum of money when her mother died. It was said her mother saved every penny she earned for Rose. She too was in the retail business, taught herself to read and write, and when the owner was out she looked at receipts and practiced reading the names and addresses. She worked in the back, cutting the material to size for dresses and fancy garments then bagging them for wealthy clients. She couldn't do too much; her legs were ridden with eczema so badly she could hardly stand, but she never missed a day from work.

The boutique was originally owned by a wealthy black woman. The story goes that her complexion was so fair she passed for a white woman. To buy the property she posed as one. After she signed the papers, paid in cash and had the papers in her hand, as she was about the leave the bank, she took off her sunglasses and head scarf, took the bobby pins out of her hair and shook it from side to side revealing her long, kinky black hair. The woman who had just sold her the boutique almost had a heart attack because she never realized she was black, but that was many moons ago and the older folks still talk about it today with pride.

*

It had been six months since Emma started working for Ms. Rose. One particular morning Ms. Rose met Emma at the entrance to the boutique.

"Good morning, Miss. Emm, hope you are well this morning, I would like to take you for breakfast, so we can talk."

"Is everything all right, Ms. Rose?" asked Emma, somewhat concerned.

"Everything is just fine, Sugar."

She hooked her arm in Emma's as they left the boutique and walked a block to the coffee shop on the corner. You would think someone of her age couldn't walk that far, but she had more pep in her step than Emma.

"Here we are," she said.

There were two people in front of them as they approached the coffee shop. The waiter seated them then he returned to seat Ms. Rose and Emma.

"Those window seats would be fine, son," Ms. Rose said to the waiter.

"What are you doing here, Grandma?" the waiter asked, embarrassed.

Ms. Rose spoke with a stern, but sweet, voice.

"Son, if you don't show me to those window seats, you will be very embarrassed." She turned to Emma and said, "That's my grandson, Aimari (pronounced Emery), his mother named him that because she loved how the English spoke and it sounded so gallant. She herself spoke nothing but the Queen's English, although never visited England until her late thirties."

Her grandson looked at Emma and smiled, then showed them to the window seats that were vacant, around a small rectangular table. Ms. Rose looked at Aimari and smiled.

"Thank you."

Emma said thank you too.

"What can I get for you lovely ladies?" Aimari said, taking his notepad out.

"Strawberry herbal tea, please, Aimari," Ms. Rose ordered, snickering.

"Now, Grandma, you know we only serve special flavored coffees."

You could see Aimari getting somewhat irritated and red to the cheeks.

"Okay, son, I'll have a coffee with vanilla, whipped cream, caramel and powered chocolate on top."

"Anything else?"

"Yes, a slice of coffee cake, please."

"Would that be all?"

"For now," she said, closing the menu without looking at it.

"And you, pretty lady?" said Aimari, with a big smile on his face.

"The same please."

"Her name is Emma, not pretty lady," Ms. Rose intervened.

"*Everything?*" Aimari said, with a surprised look on his face.

"Yes please."

He looked up at the ceiling, rolling his eyes, turned and walked toward the counter to place the orders. He came back and asked if they preferred the cake hot or cold, they both said warm at the same time, and laughed.

As Ms. Rose and Emma sat at the table looking out through the window, the old lady kept looking at Emma, making her very nervous and uncomfortable. She began talking in that soft tone voice of hers.

"Do I make you nervous, Miss Emm?"

"Not normally," Emma replied nervously, contradicting the tremble in her voice, "but today you do," she said softly, almost in a whisper.

Aimari brought the order to them and placed it on the table along with the check. They both thanked him. He left to attend to other customers waiting to be seated. Emma and Ms. Rose ate their slice of cake and drank their coffee. When finished, Ms. Rose sat back in the chair.

"That was a lovely breakfast, don't you agree, Miss Emm?"

"Oh, yes," Emma said, smiling, taking the paper napkin from her lap and wiping the corners of her mouth, as though she just eaten a big lunch.

Before she could sip the last drop of coffee, Ms. Rose casually spoke again.

"Now, let's talk."

She looked serious.

"Okay, let's talk," Emma repeated, propping herself up straight in the chair, and preparing herself for whatever it was Ms. Rose wanted to talk about.

"You're a smart girl, Emma, much like your..."

Ms. Rose stopped, leaving a curious look on Emma's face.

"I can see you going places, places you never dreamed of, gaining positions you only thought you could hold. You're going to meet people only princes and princesses meet, mark my words, young lady."

Emma was lost for words; she didn't know what to say.

"You see that building over there, the tall glass one?"

Ms. Rose pointed to the MB Design Company building.

"Yes."

She couldn't help but see it; it was the tallest building in that part of downtown.

"Well... a dear friend of mine owns the company." She looked down at her hands as she spoke, admiring her wedding band.

"Just had these diamonds polished, you know," she said, changing the subject completely.

Emma wanted to hear more about her friend, but dared not say anything. Ms. Rose never continued to speak on the subject.

"Let's go, Miss. Emm, breakfast is over."

She took a $50 bill from her purse and placed it under the used coffee cup, she pushed her chair back and stood up. Emma got up and buttoned her jacket.

"Ready?"

"Ready," Emma replied, although still startled that she had left her hanging in mid-sentence.

She hooked her arm in Emma's as she had done when they walked. As they approached the door, Aimari gave Ms. Rose a kiss on the cheek, she whispered something in his ear and he looked over to where they had been seated. He smiled and mimed, 'thank you'.

As they walked back to the boutique arm in arm, Ms. Rose was very quiet. Emma tried to make small talk, but she just chuckled without a response. When they arrived at the boutique, Ms. Rose turned to Emma.

"Miss. Emm, it's such a lovely day today, why don't you take the day off? I'm going to make a few phone calls then call it a day myself."

She patted the back of Emma's hand as she released her arm. She unlocked the door to the boutique, walked in and closed the door behind her. Emma was lost for words. She stood outside the boutique for a while, which may have been only a few seconds, but seemed like hours, before walking to her car.

*

The next morning Emma arrived at the boutique early as usual, to find Ms. Rose was already there folding the new garments and placing them on shelves.

"Good morning, Ms. Rose," Emma said, waiting for Ms. Rose to tell her not to take off her coat.

"Good morning, Miss. Emm, hope you had a wonderful day yesterday," she said, smiling.

"Yes, I did thank you, I did nothing aside from play checkers with my Aunt Lou."

"Oh, how is the ole…"

She stopped.

"You know my Aunt Lou?" Emma asked, remembering a previous conversation with her aunt.

"Why no, Miss. Emm, but I've heard you talk about her enough over the past six months, I feel as though I do," she responded, as she kept folding the new silk scarves and wrapping them in individual tissue paper according to the scarf colors then placing them on shelves.

"Okay," Emma said as she took off her coat, not believing for one minute they didn't know each other.

"Miss. Emm, I hope you don't think me forward, but I've arranged an interview for you at MB Design Company, for this afternoon at two o'clock."

She made no eye contact with Emma, but just spoke and folded at the same time. Emma spoke with a little edge to her voice. "I wish you had asked to me first, Ms. Rose."

"Would you have told me not to make the call?"

"No, but… I'm not dressed for an interview," Emma said, looking down at herself.

"Miss. Emm, you work for a boutique, please don't make excuses, if you're scared just say so."

Ms. Rose stopped what she was doing and walked toward

Emma. She reached out her hand taking hold of Emma's right hand and placing it between hers. She just stood in front of Emma and looked at her.

"I can always call and cancel, if that's what you'd like me to do, Miss. Emm."

"No, Ms. Rose, I'm very grateful," whispered Emma.

"Miss. Emm, do you remember the conversation yesterday over coffee, when I told you, you would be going places and meeting people you have only dreamed of meeting?"

"Yes," Emma said, looking at Ms. Rose.

"Well, now's the time."

She patted Emma's hand then released it and walked away.

"Don't be afraid to venture out, Miss. Emm, it's a big world out there and you're ready for the experience," Ms. Rose said, with an enormous level of confidence in Emma.

"What's the position for, Ms. Rose?"

She waved her hand and continued walking toward the back, heading for the office. As Emma was about to follow her, a customer came into the boutique.

"Good morning, how can I help you?" Emma said, hoping Ms. Rose had heard the door.

"I'm here to see Ms. Rose, the agency sent me to interview for the sales assistant's position," the young lady replied, handing Emma the sheet of paper she had in her hand from the agency.

"Okay, take a seat, I'll find Ms. Rose for you."

Emma smiled and went to the back to locate her. Ms. Rose began talking before Emma could tell her there was someone there to see her.

"Don't say a word, Miss. Emm, things will work out for you. I'm expecting a few young ladies this morning, and I hope I find one with all the wit you have."

Emma took a deep breath, and followed Ms. Rose to the front. She greeted the young lady and took her to the back. The morning continued like that; one interview after another. Emma looked at the time, it was one o'clock. She felt her hands getting sweaty and her heart racing.

Ms. Rose, periodically looking up and smiling at Emma, could see she was getting very nervous and kept looking at the clock.

"Miss. Emm, there's a navy blue suit, white shirt and the works, hung up in the back, I think you'll find they're your size," she called out to her.

Emma didn't even ask how she knew her size. She said thank you and gave her a hug. It was a perfect fit.

"How do I look?" Emma said, turning around.

"Unemployed, if you don't get moving," she said sarcastically.

"Okay, see you when I get back."

Ms. Rose chuckled.

*

Emma arrived at the MB Design Building at 1:45 P.M. She walked up to the reception desk and gave the receptionist her name. She asked her to take a seat and someone would be down to meet her in a few minutes.

As Emma sat there she looked around, admiring the marble floor entrance and glass elevators, which she presumed led to the various offices that were listed on the information wall along with pictures of senior partners. She stood up to take a closer look at the pictures, when someone spoke.

"Emma."

She turned around and a tall, dark handsome man with braids was looking straight at her.

"I'm sorry, I hope I didn't startle you, my name is Greg," he said, extending his hand.

"Emma," she said, shaking his hand.

"Shall we?" he said, pointing to the elevator.

"Please lead," Emma replied, smiling.

Greg pressed the elevator button as they waited for it to arrive on the ground floor. Emma could feel him staring at her through the mirrored walls around the elevator. She tried not to notice, but as she looked up, their eyes met, they both laughed, just then the elevator doors opened. He pressed the button for the ninth floor.

"You will be interviewed by a panel of senior partners," Greg said, starting a conversation.

"Will Mr. Brown be there also?" she asked inquiringly.

"No, Mr. Brown travels the world and generates business," Greg replied in his deep baritone voice.

"Have you met him?" another curious question.

"No, not in person, but he never forgets birthdays, the Christmas bonus and profit share. When the business has met all its yearly goals, we reap the rewards. Mr. Brown is very adamant about keeping staff happy. Here we are, Emma, take a seat, we'll call you." Greg walked toward what looked like a conference room.

I didn't ask what I am being interviewed for, Emma thought to herself when he left.

"Emma," someone called.

Emma answered, surprised to be called so soon.

"Yes."

"We're ready for you," a female voice said.

She stood up, took a deep breath and walked toward the room.

"Hello." she said as she entered the room.

"Please, take a seat," the young lady stated.

There were two suited women and three well-tailored men seated around the table, one of whom was Greg. Each had what seemed like a questionnaire sheet. Emma could feel her heart start pounding.

"Emma, let me introduce the team of partners to you. My name is Conner, senior vice president, these are Naomi, Yaz, Taylor and Greg, all senior partners."

"Nice to meet you all," Emma said, amazed they were all African-American.

"Tell me a little about yourself," said Conner.

Emma began with her completing her first year of college while still in high school, and graduating from college six months shy of her twentieth birthday in an accelerated program, with a Bachelor and Masters Degree in business administration and fashion, then continuing with her present position at Ms. Rose's boutique.

"What experience do you have in the fashion industry?" asked Yaz.

"I'm familiar with the different types of fabric, color, weight, stitching, threads and makeup, and I have a good eye for putting fashion together itself."

Emma looked around the table for expressions, hoping she had answered the question appropriately.

"What do you know about fashion shoots?" Taylor asked.

"First and foremost are location and lighting, each has to complement the other and both have to complement the product."   Emma felt confident in her response to that question.

"The position is for a marketing director, working exclusively with fashion for the cover of our three current magazines and centerfolds; the successful candidate will be responsible for setting up photo shoots at various locations, getting a production team together, choosing the models and making print decisions that will sell our magazines. Currently we have a private marketing company, but recently we were informed via e-mail from Mr. Brown that we will no longer be using that firm. We will be adding a new marketing department to MB Design Company. Do you think you can manage such a department?" asked Naomi, leaning toward Emma across the table.

Before she could respond, Greg intervened.

"I noticed your age is twenty isn't it?"

"Last week." Emma replied, wondering what her age had to do with anything.

"Happy belated birthday," Greg said, smiling.

"This is a huge responsibility. The magazines are sixty percent of this company's profit, and being a new department here in the MB building there are a few adjustments that need to be made without losing productivity - this is a mammoth task. The private firm will continue the shoots until the end of the month, and after that we will take over. My question to you, in referring to your age, is that there is no room for error, and I know young adults such as yourself these days like to party-"

Emma interrupted,

"Before you go any further, Greg, with all due respect, I am one young adult who does not like to party, as you so put it. I have earned what I have by sheer determination and persistence, hoping to become the CEO of my own fashion company one day. To answer your question and to respond to yours, Naomi, yes, I am ready for the challenge. I may be young, but I'm also enthusiastic, energetic and ready to go, and will not settle for anything less than perfect. I too have no room for errors."

Emma stared Greg in the eyes with her response, to let it be known she would not be intimidated by anyone, remembering the teachings from Ms. Rose. Conner stood up and extended his hand.

"Welcome to MB Design, Emma, I look forward to seeing what you have."

"Likewise myself," said Naomi.

"Welcome," echoed Taylor and Yaz.

"I look forward to working with you," said Greg, placing the papers in front of him in a blue folder and returning his silver pen to his inside jacket pocket.

"We will have the eighth floor cleared for you by the morning. You may choose any of the offices for yourself, my recommendation is the east wing, it overlooks the designated parking lot, but it also has a spectacular view of the park in the distance. The third floor is used for meetings, however, we are currently renovating a few of the empty offices to make a studio for you and your production team, for sample garments as well as changing rooms for the models. I presume you have an assistant in mind?" Conner said, looking through some papers he had in front of him.

Emma felt slightly shaken by his question.

"No, I don't."

"Well, we can have a temp come in tomorrow, to help you get started."

Tomorrow, Emma thought, but...

"That sounds good," she said, extending her hand to Conner.

"Your salary will be discussed with me in the morning, when you sign the company policies, terms and conditions, ethics and code of conduct. You will also receive a company handbook. Good luck, and I look forward to seeing you in the morning. Please tell Ms. Rose thank you for her recommendation - good choice," Conner said with a smile, before leaving the conference room with Naomi, Yaz and Taylor following him, leaving Greg and Emma behind.

Emma pushed her chair back, placed both hands on the table and leaned forward with the motion to stand, when Greg struck up a conversation. He made no effort to move, he sat there relaxed in his seat.

"Are you any relation to Ms. Rose?"

"No, I work in her boutique that's about all."

Emma sat back down in her seat, as Greg indicated by pushing his seat back, crossing his legs, putting his hands behind his head and tilting the chair back, that he wanted to talk. Emma sat down, her chair was already pushed back and she too crossed her legs, which made her skirt rise, revealing a little too much leg, but with sophistication she reached for her purse and placed it on her lap.

"You don't have to cover them up you know."

"Cover what up?"

"Those long shapely legs of yours."

"Greg... do you always compliment ladies on their legs?" Emma asked, thinking him a little forward.

"If I see a pair I like I do."

Emma changed the subject before things got out of hand.

"Can you show me the eighth floor offices before I leave, please?"

"Certainly, we can use the back elevator."

"I'd rather use the front one... if you don't mind," Emma said, giving him a look.

"Your choice," Greg said with a smirk, fixing his tie.

They left through the same door they had entered earlier and used the same elevator to go to the eighth floor. When the elevator doors slid open on the eighth floor, there was a lot of furniture sitting there waiting to be moved, covered with white sheets.

"Wow, they move fast," Greg said, surprised.

"Who moves fast?" Emma responded, wanting to know.

"The graphic designers; they occupied this floor, now they're moving to the sixth floor, and marketing, as you know, will be here."

"Why didn't they just give me the sixth floor?" Emma asked, trying to make sense of the move.

"Because the office spaces are bigger on the eighth floor."

"Why would I need such a big office?"

"You need all the space you can get for your new production team, they need space for layout of materials, samples etc."

"But I thought that's what the third floor was being renovated for."

"No, the third floor is being renovated for fittings, sample garments, in-house fashion shoots and basically so you can see what you have to work with before print and fashion shows."

"Oh, I see," said Emma, with a bewildered expression on her face.

"Don't look so puzzled; it will all fall into place, you'll see," Greg said, sounding the perfect gentleman.

As they walked through the offices, Emma was stunned at the décor in all the suites. Each suite had one wall with a ceiling to floor mirror, and the rest were in a rich wood texture in oak. The floors had a grey marble color twelve by twelve tiles that were absolutely gorgeous. The ceiling was white with sunken light fixtures.

"This is the office Conner recommended," said Greg as they approached the east wing.

"Oh, my God, this is spectacular!" Emma exclaimed in amazement. "What is that area for?" she asked, pointing to the area outside her office as they entered through the glass double doors.

"That area is for your assistant," said Greg. "Each assistant has their own suite adjacent to their boss, it just makes life a little easier, and they will know when you're in or out."

"Doesn't that invade their privacy a little?" Emma whispered.

"No, Emm, do you mind if I call you Emm?"

"No, please do."

"Your assistant should be your right-hand person, you should have every reason to be confident with them. If you have the slightest doubt, don't keep them. See, you are the key to what's next in fashion, and we don't want anything leaking out before we go public."

"Oh, I see, is that why Conner asked me if I had an assistant in mind?"

"That's the reason; Trust... with a capital 'T'."

"Greg... can you help me out? I don't have anyone in mind, can you recommend someone?"

"I thought you'd never ask," Greg said, willing to help.

"Great," Emma said, feeling more relaxed.

"Let's go to my office, I have a resume folder you can take a look at for your production team and assistant. There are some very talented people out there, all waiting to join MB Design."

Emma was a bit apprehensive going to Greg's office, and it showed on her face

"Where is your office?"

"On the ninth floor, is there a problem? If there is, I can bring the folder down to you in the lobby if that makes you feel more comfortable," Greg said genuinely.

"No, that's all right, if we're going to be working together, what better time than the present to get to know each other," Emma said bravely.

Emma and Greg left the empty offices on the eighth floor and took the elevator back up to the ninth floor.

"How did you make senior partner?" Emma said, striking up a conversation to relax herself.

"Well, I used to model for a few of MB magazines. One day I came in to pick up some sample pictures from Conner and ended up having a conversation with him. He asked my age, at the time I was twenty-one. He explained modeling was only a phase job, once you hit twenty-five, younger more handsome men take over and you're left struggling for a paycheck. He proceeded to tell me they were creating a new department for male models, which included the MB male clothing line, and they needed a manager to oversee the project - and who knew more about modeling? He left the question open. That was nineteen years ago and I haven't looked back since."

"Any regrets?"

"None."

"My office is on the right, let me get the door for you."

The more Emma spoke with Greg the more she liked his style, he was very suave and twenty years her senior. He gave her the folder of resumes to look through. She had to somehow make a selection to interview by the following day. Emma thanked him and told him she looked forward to seeing him the next morning.

It was getting late and Emma rushed back to Ms. Rose's boutique, hoping she hadn't left yet. As she approached the door, she saw the lights were still on. Thank God, she said to herself.

"Ms. Rose," she yelled, "Ms. Rose."

"Why are you yelling, Miss. Emm? You know I'm not far."

"I got the job, Ms. Rose, how can I ever thank you?"

Emma gave her a big hug, she could feel the tears welling up in her eyes.

"I know you're not crying, Miss. Emm, this is a great opportunity for you. You can thank me by being successful. Now, go home, get a good night's rest, you have a big day tomorrow."

"Wait... how did you know I start tomorrow?" Emma said, curious.

"I'm a wise old woman, Miss. Emm, when I know someone is ready they are just ready."

Emma gave her another hug then walked out of the boutique.

*

When she arrived home that evening, something strange came over her; she couldn't relax, she felt anxious, as though she was choking, she needed fresh air. She called out to Aunt Lou, letting her know she was going for a drive, she needed to get out. She found herself driving to the other side of town, and stopped at Harry's Motel for some reason. She got out of her car. As she approached the lobby, the man at the front desk asked her:

"One hour or two?"

She knew what she was doing, but subconsciously she couldn't stop herself.

"Two," she said quietly.

"That'll be one hundred and fifty bucks."

"One hundred and fifty bucks," Emma repeated.

"Yeah, one hundred and fifty bucks cash, you got something wrong with your ears?"

"No."

"Huh, first time, eh? Don't worry, first time is always the hardest."

He was a grubby old man, white with silver-gray hair, unshaven beard, chubby, with a cigar in his mouth. He had a high-pitched rough voice. He gave Emma the keys to room three hundred and eleven. Perhaps this wasn't a good idea after all, she thought to herself, maybe I should just leave.

She took the elevator to the third floor, and as she was about to pull the key out of the keyhole and turn back, she heard the elevator stop on that floor. She quickly turned the key, rushed into the room and stood behind the door as if being chased by someone. What are you doing? she said to herself, acting like a crazy person. Just then someone knocked on the door. She said nothing, but held her breath, they knocked again. She peeped through the spy hole and saw a woman standing there.

"Oh God, oh God," she kept saying. "What am I doing?"

Emma was panicking. There was a third knock, this time the person spoke.

"You gonna pay me anyway, not like I going anywhere."

Emma opened the door slightly and peeped through the

crack.

"I'm sorry, how much do I owe you?" Emma said, scared as could be.

The woman looked at her, chewing gum.

"Let me in and I'll tell ya."

Emma started shaking as she pulled the door back to let her in.

"Scared?"

"Yes, I am," Emma said, shaking.

"What is a pretty little thing like you doing in this neck of the hood?"

"I'm not sure, I guess, I guess I wanted to experience it with someone I'd never see again," Emma said quietly.

"Wanted to experience what?"

"You know."

"No, I don't know, tell me."

Emma could not bring herself to say the words, 'experience with another woman', because she was not sure of her sexuality. She felt different inside when she was close to women. However, after meeting Greg she felt a twisting sensation in the pit of her stomach, which had her all confused.

"I thought I liked women," she said, ashamed, and walked toward the bed and sat down. She put her elbows on her knees and put her head down in her cupped hands. "I'm such a fool, so… confused, so… silly," she said, sobbing.

"So, where you from?" asked the woman, paying no attention to Emma's emotional state.

"The other side of town," Emma said, wiping her nose on the cuff of her sleeve.

"Where?" the woman continued, sounding a little aggressive.

"Not far… about forty-five minutes from here."

"Girl… you are confused to drive forty-five minutes to find out you're not gay," said the woman, looking at Emma, raising her eyebrows. "Neither am I," she continued. "This is one of Ma Bell's places, she sent me to see chubby downstairs for work, and he sent me to three eleven, looks like we're both confused… I need the money and you need to find out who you is."

What kind of language is she speaking? Emma asked herself.

"What a night." The woman sighed, walking to sit beside Emma. "By the way, my name is Karen J," she said, extending her hand.

"Emma."

"What kinda name is Emma… you white? Don't answer that, girl, I'm just messing with ya." Karen started laughing. "Now, wipe your face and blow your nose, in fact go wash your face… you half-white folks get red like someone done slap the-"

"Okay, I get it," said Emma, before Karen could finish her sentence.

Emma raised her head and looked up at Karen, they both laughed. Emma got up and washed her face then returned and sat on the bed next to Karen. The two joked and made complete fools of themselves. Before they knew it, chubby was knocking at the door telling them their time was up. Emma totally forgot she had to review the resumes.

"It was nice meeting you," Emma said sincerely. "I don't think I've laughed so much since leaving high school... thank you," she said, walking toward her silver Honda.

"When was that, yesterday?" Karen said, with a sad look on her face as though she was losing her best friend.

"It seems like it," Emma responded. "Listen, Karen, what are you doing tomorrow, say about two o'clock?"

"Nothing."

"Okay, meet me at this address." Emma wrote the address to MB Design on a piece of paper and gave it to her. "Oh, do you have anything other than that to wear?"

"See, I knew you were white, you didn't have to go there," Karen said all ghettoish, rolling her head.

"I didn't mean it like that..." Emma said, correcting herself. "Call this number and ask for Ms. Rose, tell her Miss. Emma sent you, just say navy blue suit and the works, she'll understand. One more thing, leave the ghetto here, please."

Emma gave Karen, her last $100 bill. She took it so fast and placed it between her breasts that Emma looked at her and raised her eyebrows. She gestured 'what?' by her head and hand movement.

Three

"Let me guess, you must be Emma Trent," said the attractive woman behind the reception desk.

"Yes, I am, but..." said Emma.

"Oh, don't look surprised, honey; all new employees are screened before being employed at MB, that's what makes them so successful. Pam, by the way."

She extended her hand to Emma over the desk.

"I don't remember seeing you when I came for the interview yesterday," Emma said, looking at her.

"No... I had a doctor's appointment."

"I hope it's nothing serious."

"No, routine girl stuff, you know," said Pam.

Pam was the manager for the front desk. She was medium height, sporting a long, straight black weave with a center parting, she had dark smooth skin, light brown eyes, Emma couldn't tell if they were contacts or not, a beautiful smile and full lips, her make-up was immaculate. Pam, an older woman, was full figured and well endowed on top. When she came from behind the counter to straighten the magazines and put the day's newspaper on the coffee tables, she was working that uniform. The navy blue, fitted single-breasted jacket, with the MB logo engraved on the left lapel, with light blue scalloped bust line, spandex short-sleeved shirt and knee-length fitted skirt with a small slit in the back, and those three-inch heel black pumps completed the look. Emma was later told that it looked more professional for the receptionists to have the same look, the navy blue and light blue were the colors of choice instead of the traditional blue and white.

"It's a pleasure meeting you, Pam."

"Likewise, Miss Trent."

"Oh, please call me Emma, or Emm, I only use my last name when I have to."

"Why, you should be proud of your parents' name," said Pam, giving Emma the 'you're still young' look.

"It's not that," Emma said, trying to defend her statement, "but... when I was in school, they used to tease me by calling me ET because of my initials Emma T. Trent."

"What's the middle T for, if you don't mind me asking?"

"Tiara. My aunt told me, when I was born my mom said one day I'll wear a crown and be a queen of my own domain and have the key to the world."

"Strong words, your mother must be a very strong lady."

"Why lady, and not woman?" Emma said.

"I look at you and I don't know you, but I can see you came from something no woman would raise, you were raised by a lady... Come here, let me show you something."

Pam walked Emma over to the mirrored wall.

"Look at yourself, take a good look, you see how you're dressed; full tailored red suit, white lace blouse, no cleavage showing, hair pinned up into a French twist, natural color make-up, single, I know you're God-fearing, I can see it in your eyes. Emma, be the strong lady your mother intended you to be, now go to your office, folks have started coming in."

Pam walked back over to the reception area, whilst Emma continued looking at herself in the mirror and for some reason said: "Tiara Trent, you are a lady."

She pressed the button for the elevator and waited. Before it arrived, Pam called out.

"Do you have any boxes or anything you'd like taken up to your office?"

"Just me, but I'm expecting a Karen Jenkins at two o'clock this afternoon," Emma replied.

"Okay, I'll put her name on the log."

"Thank you."

"I'll call you when she arrives."

Emma was somewhat reluctant to go up to the office, thinking it may not be ready. It looked like there was so much to do last night. She walked away from the elevator area and took a seat in the lobby. How did Pam know I was single? she thought.

Pam saw Emma take a seat, and came over to her.

"Is everything all right?"

"Yes," she replied, "I don't think the office is ready yet, so I'll just sit here for a while."

Pam chuckled.

"What's so funny?" Emma said, looking up at her as she stood over her.

"I didn't mean to laugh, but, all the suites on the eighth floor are fully furnished and waiting to be occupied."

"But… last evening before I left they were empty, and boxes were all over the place," said Emma, surprised.

"MB works magic overnight," Pam said in a whisper, leaning over her. "Mr. Brown, who before you ask, I've never met, insists all the suites have identical furniture; it saves time and no one has to argue about color, blue for boys pink for girls, that sort of thing, you know what I mean?"

"Yes. I do… Thank you, Pam, I'll head on up to my office then."

As Emma turned toward the elevator, she heard someone say:

"Hold the elevator, please."

She recognized the voice.

"Well, you're bright and early."

"Is that good or bad?" she asked, trying not to make eye

contact with Greg.

"Wait up," another voice said.

"Whew! I thought I'd missed the elevator," said Yaz, all out of breath from running.

"We would have waited," said Greg.

Yaz gave him a look, which Emma pretended not to see.

"I'm sure you would have," Yaz mumbled.

"Welcome again, Emma, I can see by your attire you have class."

"Thank you," she said, with a big smile on her face.

Just then, Yaz's cell phone started ringing.

"Uh-oh, what have I done?" Yaz said, looking at her caller ID. "It's Conner," she said, looking at them. "Good morning, Conner, how are you?" Yaz said, putting on a voice. "Coffee, you didn't say anything about coffee, for when?" Yaz paused. "This morning, and now you're telling me, Conner."

You could tell by the change in tone and up-tempo that Yaz was not happy.

"He's... he's... such a ..." Yaz stopped, her expression said it all. She looked at Greg and Emma through the mirror in the elevator and smiled. "I'm taking the elevator back down then I'm going to the specialty coffee shop to get the specially flavored pre-ordered coffees for an 8:00 A.M. meeting *this* morning in Conner's office, with the new prospective clients, so there goes my morning yoga." Before the elevator doors closed, Yaz, yelled, "You both need to be there."

Greg looked at the sliding elevator door.

"Did she say what I thought she said?"

"Yes, she did."

Greg got off on the eighth floor to escort Emma to her new office and give her the official MB welcome, and also to go over some of the resumes he had given her the previous evening. Emma started laughing silently to herself, hoping Greg didn't see, remembering something from the previous night, but Greg *did* see.

"What are you laughing about?"

"Oh, nothing."

"So, you laugh at nothing?"

"No, it was something I remember from last night."

"Care to share?"

"No, not really."

"Okay, it's your personal joke, ha ha," Greg said, probably feeling uncomfortable.

As they approached her new office Emma was thrilled.

"This is wonderful!" she exclaimed, trying to change the mood. "They did all this in one night?"

"You'll be surprised what MB can change in one night," Greg said with a flirtatious tone.

"Pam is a wonderful woman," Emma said, changing the subject even further.

"*Missss* Pam," Greg said, shaking his head and dragging out Miss as though something was wrong with her.

"Why Miss Pam and the long *Missss*?" Emma said, mocking him.

"You have to know Pam in order to *know* Pam," he replied, making quotation marks with his fingers

"Uh-oh," Emma said, feeling curious, placing her purse on the desk. "Tell me what I need to know," she said, folding her arms.

"Listen, I don't mean to cut you, but... meet you in the conference room, ninth floor, eight o'clock," Greg said, dashing through the doorway trying to catch the elevator.

Emma shook her head and smiled. Oh, boy, this is going to be a fun day, she thought. She walked toward the window to take in the spectacular view. Conner was right; the east wing had all the view of the parking garage surrounded by park benches, and in the distance she could see the trees in the park. I bet this must be so picturesque in the winter, Emma thought. As she was about to turn and walk back to her desk, she noticed a woman sitting on a bench. It was at a distance, but it was clearly a woman. Emma thought it odd; maybe she was taking a morning stroll or something.

Emma dismissed the thought from her head, walked back to her desk and pulled out the high-backed, brown, leather executive chair, which still had the plastic on it. She pulled the plastic off, exposing that strong leather scent. The desk was a rich maple color, high-grade wood, large, almost centered in the office, but not quite. To her left was a wall-to-wall, ceiling to floor unit with several compartments, and to her right a wall-to-wall credenza and a centered flat screen television on the wall. To the left of the television on the credenza was a glass cabinet displaying many MB awards and trophies. Emma felt so honored and excited that Mr. Brown wanted them displayed in her office.

"Oh, my God, the meeting!" Emma whispered.

She had been so busy getting comfortable she had forgotten about the meeting. She rushed toward the elevator, taking her notepad and pen. She pressed the button. The elevator seemed like it was taking forever to get there, and when it did, to her surprise, as the door opened she was fixing my skirt. When she looked up, there was Conner.

"Good morning, Emma, how are you settling in?"

"Nicely, thank you."

She wished she could just dig a hole and fall into it. Emma entered the elevator, holding her notepad across her chest.

"After you," Conner said as the elevator doors opened on the ninth floor. "This way, Emma, we're using the large conference room this morning."

"Oh, thank you."

Emma felt a bit lost heading for the conference room where she had been interviewed the previous day.

"Don't worry, this was short notice for you, usually you'll be given ample notice of all meetings conducted with potential clients," Conner said, reaching out, showing her the way.

Conner was an older man, tall, caramel skin tone, brown eyes, salt and pepper well-groomed hair, masculine body, deep voice. He wore a grey tailored suit with a red tie and light grey shirt, snakeskin grey and black shoes. Oh, he has a wedding band, Emma thought. His expression was serious.

"Good morning," Conner began. "Before I introduce you to our new prospective clients, I would like to welcome Miss Emma Trent once again to MB Design, and our first of many meetings as the new marketing director, should she decide to stay with us at MB." Everyone clapped and welcomed her again.

"To begin, I'd like to go over the proposals…"

The meeting lasted until 11:30 A.M., by which time Emma was starving; she could not wait until Conner officially adjourned the meeting. When he did, it was meeting and greeting time. Emma tried to slip away as the clients were leaving. As she headed for the door, seeing her escape, Conner announced:

"An overview lunch."

What is that? she thought, turning on her heel to face him as he watched the clients leave the room.

"Ask Telloris if she wouldn't mind bringing the menus to that quaint little restaurant across the parking garage for us, please, Naomi," Conner said.

Naomi picked up the phone and paged Telloris to come to the conference room. Emma asked Conner what an overview lunch was. He explained in full detail.

"An overview lunch is when all the senior partners get together after the initial proposal meeting, which we had this morning, and go over it in depth, pulling apart the proposals then analyzing words and meanings, making sure they are used in the right context, and so on and so forth."

"But I'm not a partner," Emma said, hoping he would excuse her.

"I want you to understand how all meetings are conducted, and in the overview lunch, you'll understand there is a philosophy behind this concept," he said.

"But didn't we just go through the proposal with the clients?" asked Emma, thinking it would be double work.

"Yes, we did just go through, now it's time to analyze before we sign."

"I don't understand." said Emma.

"That's why I want you here."

Everyone ordered a different wrap sandwich from the menu Telloris brought to the conference room. Conner asked everyone to get comfortable and look over the proposals with a fine toothcomb.

"This could be a million dollar deal, think of your bonuses, make sure every detail is understood, we don't need any surprises when we go to closing," he added.

Telloris made copies of the three proposals and took the originals with her as she left the conference room. Each of the partners took a copy, went to various parts of the room, made themselves comfortable and began reading. Emma noticed each of them taking a notepad from some boxes Telloris had placed on the table, each with different letters on them. She stood there a little confused. She waited for Conner to finish his phone call then asked him what she should do, seeing as none of the other partners had bothered to tell her.

"I'm sorry, Emma, let me explain the concept. If there seems to be a discrepancy with what was said verbally in the meeting this morning to what is written in the proposal, we take a HDBR notepad and write the difference."

"What is HDBR?"

"My apologies, these are some terminologies we use at MB; for instance, each proposed meeting is recorded and later transcribed. When you go through the proposal and compare it with the transcript it must match. If the client has written, 'We will use spandex throughout' in the proposal, but in the meeting transcribed they verbally state, 'We will use spandex mix throughout', then that calls for a HDBAR card, which stands for 'Highlight, Discuss, Bring to Attention and Resolve'. We highlight the section in the proposal likewise the section from the transcript, it is brought to the client's attention then we resolve, in each area of discrepancy we HDBAR."

"What are the other letters for?" Emma asked, already sounding confused.

"At the end of each discrepancy, you attach a CMCIW card, which is 'Client Must Confirm in Writing'. This is extremely important; if silk is spelled wrong you place a CSE card, which is 'Client Spelling Error'. At the end of each overview, Telloris is then given all the notes. She draws up a CMRM, which is 'Client Must Revise Memo', noting the discrepancies, and the memo is then routed to each of you for review. The final stage is to send the original proposal back to the potential client, along with a copy of the transcript and the memo outlining the discrepancies. It is vital that all proposed clients are aware that the meetings are being recorded and an acknowledgement slip must be signed prior to the start of any meeting. Pam will electronically send the acknowledgement slips directly to the conference rooms upon their arrival. Any potential client who refuses to sign will not go any farther than the lobby."

"This is a lot to take in," said Emma.

"It's your first day, in six months this will be as natural as making a cup of coffee," said Conner, having total confidence in her.

"If you say so," Emma said, trying to convince herself.

"Any meetings you set up must be cleared with Pam, so there are no conflicts with conference room time."

"Okay."

Emma was overwhelmed and felt herself giving up before she had started, but the words of Ms. Rose came flooding to her mind; 'Wealth is not seen'. She looked around the conference room from Conner to Naomi and she could not tell or see wealth, but she knew they all acquired it, or they would not be there.

Yaz was very vocal. Emma thought she might still be upset from that morning. She had some good points, and Conner noted them and winked at her. Yaz, short for Yazmyne, was of mixed race; her father was black African and her mother white from South Africa. She spoke with a beautiful accent, however that changed when she was upset, as Emma had witnessed that morning. She was tall, fair complexion, pretty light brown eyes almost marble-like, full lips, curly short hair dyed a reddish color, she was also very shapely.

Emma could tell she had a thing for Greg, by the way she looked and spoke to him. It was clear when she sat next to him at the meeting that morning and kept touching his arm with her pinky finger. Emma saw, but dismissed it from her mind. They're working buddies, she convinced herself to believe.

Four

"Wow, what a day!" Emma exclaimed, resting my head on Greg's arm, taking her right shoe off. "I'm sorry," she said, catching herself, "I forgot where I was for a moment."

"Oh, don't mind me, it felt kinda good," Greg said, smiling, showing those brilliant whites.

"Karen..." Emma suddenly remembered. "What time is it?" she asked stylishly, trying not to panic, hoping it would not show.

"Three fifteen, why?" Greg asked, giving her the raised eyebrow look, then he coughed and rocked from heel to toe. "Just tell him you were in a meeting all day, being brought up to date on company policies."

"What *are* you talking about, Greg, and who is *he?*" Emma said with attitude, looking up at him as they stood side by side waiting for the elevator.

"Wow, wow, wait up, li'l sis," Greg said, backing away. "I merely suggested you tell your boo-"

"And who said I had a boo?" Emma said, pinching herself.

"You mean you don't... have a gentleman interest?"

Greg sounded very surprised fixing himself in the reflection of the elevator looking at her and smiling.

"No, I don't have a gentleman interest."

Emma repeated his words, looking back and smiling, then holding her head down a little embarrassed.

"Sorry," she said.

"Sorry for what?"

For raising my voice and acting like a child, Emma thought, avoiding his gaze.

"Forget it, we both lost ourselves for a moment, I should be the one apologizing for wanting to know your personal business."

"Okay, we're both sorry," she said, and held on to his arm as the elevator doors opened. "Where are you going?" she asked.

"I just want to make sure you get back to your office safe and sound."

"Oh, do you now?" said Emma, thankful for the company.

"Yes, I do," Greg said with that flirtatious tone again.

They stepped out of the elevator into the eighth floor lobby, heading east to her office. As they approached the swinging glass doors, she noticed the assistant's desk was complete with glass filing trays and accessories.

"This is nice; it wasn't like this when I came in this morning."

"Well, either you have an assistant or one was appointed to you."

"What do you mean?"

"The only ones who have a choice with desk accessories are the assistants, they can choose between, glass, oak or mahogany... Yours has taste, she chose glass. I thought you didn't have anyone in mind?"

"I didn't until..." Emma paused and continued into her office.

"What's the number for reception, Greg?"

"Pam's extension is 7333."

"Thank you."

She turned to face the window. As she dialed the extension she could feel Greg staring at her, his eyes burning a hole in her back.

"Send her up, Pam... Thank you," Emma said, ending the call.

"I'll leave you to it now you're safe in your office, I'll call you with my extension," he said as he walked through the glass doors heading for the elevator.

Emma felt strange to the pit of her stomach again. What was this feeling? She hoped it wasn't the sandwich she had eaten earlier. She brushed the feeling off and waited for Karen to arrive. Emma heard the elevator, and went into the lobby to meet her. As the elevator doors opened a truly glamorous woman stepped out. It could not be...

"Karen, is that you?" she whispered.

"What... you forgot what I looked like already, girl?"

"No, but... but..."

"Girl, you drop something!"

"What?"

"Your lip! Now, where dis office at?"

Karen sure knew how to make an entrance.

"Come here, girl, give me a hug," Emma said.

Emma put her arm around Karen's waist as they walked toward the office. As they went through the glass doors, Karen stopped and took a step back.

"What we doing here, girl? Why you bringing me to the boss's office, you have to coach me some."

"Coach you on what?" Emma asked, knitting her eyebrows.

"You know I ain't intelligent like you, don't embarrass me, please, just tell me what to say."

Emma could sense Karen was truly afraid; she could see the fear in her eyes.

"Karen, this is *my* office, and this is *your* area," Emma said.

"*My* area, all this, it's bigger than my grib... girl, lemme stop."

Karen was so excited. Emma opened the double doors leading into her office, Karen stood there with her mouth wide open.

"This is your office! Hold on, let me look before I wake up."

Emma laughed and walked toward the window.

"This is not a dream, Karen, it's real, girl, come here, take a look at this view."

There was no response. Emma turned around and she had gone.

"Karen... Karen."

Emma walked out of the office and saw Karen heading for the elevator.

"Where are you going?" she called, following her, but she did not reply.

"Karen, I'm talking to you, wait."

Karen stopped outside the elevator with her back still turned toward Emma,

"What is it, did I say something?"

"No, girl."

"Then why are you crying?" Emma asked, concerned.

"I don't belong in a fancy place like this, Emma, and you know that."

"Stop it, stop it right now," Emma said. She could feel herself getting angry. "I'm sick and tired of black people running away from opportunities, always putting themselves down, they can't do this, they don't belong here, then where *do* you belong? Stop holding yourself back. If you think you don't belong here then press the button, I won't try to stop you."

Emma turned and walked back toward her office. When she heard the elevator coming, she pulled the clip holding her French twist from her hair, rummaged both her hands through it and grunted as she walked faster to her office. She walked through the glass doors passing what would have been Karen's area, through the double doors leading to her office and closed them behind her. She took a deep breath and slowly walked over to the desk. She slumped into the brown leather chair, dropping both arms either side of her, pressing her head firmly into the back of chair. After composing herself, she picked up the phone and dialed Pam's extension.

"Hey, Pam, it's Emma."

"You sound like you've just lost your best friend, what can I do for you?"

"Has Karen left the building yet?"

"No, she didn't come back down here."

"Are you sure?"

"Positive."

"Okay, when she does, please ask her to reconsider the position."

"Okay, I will."

Just as Emma hung up the phone, there was a knock on the door.

"Come in," she said as though nothing was wrong.

I guess they did not hear me, she thought.

"*Come in.*"

Still no one came in. Emma tried not to panic, knowing she

was the only person on the eighth floor. She picked up the phone and dialed Pam.

"Pam."

"Why are you whispering?"

"I think someone is outside my office, when I tell them to come in, no one enters."

"I'll have security there in one minute, stay on the phone with me."

At that moment, Emma heard the elevator, and feet running toward her office.

"They should be there."

"They are, I can hear their feet."

"Okay, I've got to go, you're in safe hands now."

Just then Emma heard a commotion outside her office. She opened the door, and there was Karen and three security guards.

"You called for security, Miss?"

"Yes, I called the reception area, I guess I was nervous," said Emma.

"Do you know this woman?" another security guard said, holding Karen's arm.

"Yes, I do, she's my new assistant, it's the first day for both of us and I guess we're a little jumpy."

"Okay, we'll let it slide this time, but remember each time security is called we must file a report, you both have a nice evening."

The security guard let Karen's arm go, she looked at him and smiled.

"Well, at least you know security works," Karen said, and they both laughed and walked into Emma's office. "I thought about what you said," Karen said, holding her head down.

"Lift your head up, this is just the beginning of a beautiful thing. Talking about beginnings, let's start with names. Let's see..." Emma started walking around her office. "How about KJ?"

"KJ, who you want to call KJ?"

"*You...* short for Karen Jenkins."

"So what am I supposed to call you, *Madam*?"

"No, silly," she said, giggling. "If you'd like me to call you Karen I will."

"No, you can call me KJ, I'll get use to it, just like I'm gonna get use to this office."

"Okay, first, when we leave here tonight we're going to the book store to check out some speech tapes, I'm going to make you so refined you won't remember where you came from."

"Girl, you can't make me fine, I know I'm fine."

"I didn't say fine, I said re... never mind... let's first see how these phones work."

KJ and Emma walked out into KJ's new area. She pulled the

plastic off the high-backed, executive, black leather chair, took her shoes off, sat in the chair and swung around, just like a child would do, making that 'weee' sound. Emma just watched. She could see there was genuine joy - Emma knew she made the perfect choice.

For the remainder of the week, Emma interviewed countless individuals, trying to build a production team with the help of Greg. When they had filled the last position, Greg, KJ and Emma went out for a drink to celebrate. Of course, being under twenty-one, Emma had to settle for sparkling flavored water.

Five

"It's hard to believe we've been here almost a year, Emm," KJ said as she sat with Emma to have their morning coffee before starting the day.

"Yes, and look how much we've accomplished. I couldn't have done it without you, KJ, thank you for accepting the position."

"I'm glad you offered it to me."

"KJ, you've grown so much in the last year."

"It's like you said, Emm, new beginnings. With the generous starting salary, I'm able to put my girls through college and I've decided to go and sit the GED."

"That's great, KJ, when?"

"I would rather not say until I've taken it."

"You would rather... who is this speaking?"

KJ felt bashful, smiling with that gleam of newfound confidence.

"You'll pass first time, I believe that."

"Thank you, Emm, for everything."

"Have you made a decision on the condo, so you can move closer to this part of town?"

"No, I'm going to wait until after the holidays, maybe the

early part of the New Year."

"KJ... listen, I know you still have a little doubt in your mind that this is all a dream, but it isn't, and I have no intension of waking you up if it is, because this is one dream I want to hold on to."

KJ and Emma had a very busy few months ahead of them. So far they had been able to pull off every cover and centerfold with rave reviews, now they had to prepare for their first fashion show, a charity event to raise funds for a finishing school for girls.

It had always been a passion of Emma's for young girls to express the English language as though they were royalty, not just speaking, but also speaking with confidence and pride, giving them the seal of approval that they were somebody, and that they were the reason there was a tomorrow. The way they walked, dressed, identified themselves and commanded respect. When one can admit even their smallest fault, then we know we are making progress, the first step is always admitting.

*

"We did it, KJ, our first successful fashion show," said Emma as the last model left the stage.

"Wow, listen to the applause," KJ and Emma said excitedly.

"What a team you have, congratulations," said Conner, making a surprise appearance.

"I didn't think you were here," said Emma.

"Did you think I would miss such an event?" Conner replied.

Even on a Saturday he looks as though he has just stepped out of a magazine, Emma thought.

"By the way, this is Juliana, my wife."

"Nice to meet you, I'm Emma and this is KJ;" Emma said, finally getting to meet the woman behind that debonair man.

"Lovely show, I look forward to the next event," said Juliana.

"Thank you," replied Emma.

"I'll see you in the office on Monday," Conner said, holding Juliana's arm and giving the team the thumbs up.

"Have a pleasant evening," KJ said.

Conner and his wife walked around congratulating the production crew and models, complimenting them on a job well done. His wife, maybe in her late fifties, could have been a model herself with her tall, slender frame, short, cropped salt and pepper hair and fair complexion. Her make-up was of artistry, with berry colored lipstick. She wore a winter white pantsuit with a three-strand pearl necklace, a pink and winter white floral scarf over the left shoulder pinned with a silver and pearl brooch. They made the perfect couple.

"I deserve a drink after this," Emma said aloud to KJ.

"Yes, you do," said a voice nothing like KJ's.

"Where did *you* spring from?" asked Emma.

"That was quite a show," Greg complimented.

"Thank you."

"The first of many to come... Talking about the first of many; happy birthday, Emm."

"Greg, how did you know?"

"I've been counting the months until you were legally twenty-one."

"Why?" Emma asked, so naïve.

"Why... you ask?"

"This man has been head over heels for you since I met him," said KJ, "and don't act like you didn't know. I guess if we're celebrating I might as well tell you both, because I know he'll be around... Well, I got my GED results yesterday..."

KJ paused.

"Well, did you pass?"

KJ walked away, turning her back on Greg and Emma. Feeling for something in her purse, she took out an envelope and passed it to Emma without turning around.

"You don't have to do this, KJ."

She shook the envelope, indicating that Emma should take it from her. Emma took the envelope from KJ's hand, opened it and read the first words.

"*Dear Miss Jenkins, congratulations, you have passed your GED...*" Emma screamed, waving the letter in the air. "You passed!"

When KJ turned around, no matter how she tried she could not hide the tears.

"These are tears of joy, Emm, I couldn't have done it without you, and you have really changed my life."

"Huh. Come here, girl," said Emma. "Give me a hug."

"Is there room for me?" Greg asked, feeling left out.

"Group hug!"

Emma and KJ both extended their arms to include Greg.

"Now, I do believe I owe you both dinner tonight."

"Well I-" KJ started.

"Well I, nothing... *both* of you."

Greg looked at the two of them before Emma could say a word.

"Okay then, I'll pick KJ up at seven thirty, and then we'll pick you up at eight o'clock, is that all right?"

"That's fine," they both said.

Greg walked them to Emma's car. Emma waved to the production crew as they drove by, blowing them a kiss, indicating a job well done. Greg looked at her and bowed his head before walking toward his own car, but not before KJ and Emma got into the car and turned the key in the ignition.

"Don't let him get away, that is a fine young man," KJ said as they pulled away from the parking lot.

"I know, believe me, I know," said Emma.

"You're so mature for your age, Emm... ever had a boyfriend?"

Emma was hesitant to answer.

"No."

"*No*, a pretty girl like you never had a boyfriend, come on."

"I've never had a boyfriend, KJ, I have been too busy trying to reach my goals and be successful. I don't need a man to keep me from achieving that."

KJ looked at her out of the corner of her eye and she knew by the tone of Emma's voice she did not want to talk about it. KJ fiddled with her purse on her lap before speaking.

"Oh, one more surprise."

What can this be, Emma thought.

"I was going to wait until Monday, but I'll tell you now. I enrolled in college to get my AA. I've been carrying the application around in my purse forever, anticipating the GED results."

"That's great, KJ, really," Emma said with genuine feeling.

"Keep your eyes on the road, Emm, remember we have a double dinner date tonight, and I want to keep it."

"I hear you," Emma replied.

Six

Greg picked KJ up at seven thirty that evening as promised. He was a bit surprised at where she lived. He knocked on the door and KJ answered.

"Wow, you look like a fox!"

"People still say fox?" KJ said, laughing.

"Well, I didn't want to say anything offensive."

Greg and KJ walked toward his shiny black BMW, with black leather interior.

"This is you?"

"No, it's my car," Greg replied sarcastically.

"Don't let me have to get black on your... remember this is The Hood."

"I know... and I'd like to get out of The Hood, I can feel the eyes looking."

KJ laughed and got into the back seat of the car, leaving the front for Emma.

"This is very nice of you, Greg, I really appreciate it."

"You deserve it."

"You can talk to me, you know."

"About what?" he asked, looking back at KJ through the rear-view mirror.

"Don't you mean, about whom?"

"Well, excuse me, Miss English Teacher."

KJ held her head down, feeling a little embarrassed.

"About whom," Greg said, chuckling.

"What do you want to know? I just don't want to see her get hurt, that's all, so if you know you have others waiting in the wings, don't start something with Emma. She's twenty-one today, now she's legal, let her innocence stay until she's ready."

Greg looked at KJ through the rear-view mirror once more, but said nothing.

"What I'm saying to you, Greg, here in this car, I want to stay right here."

"You know I'm a grown man, right?" Greg responded, looking serious.

"How do you know a grown man, Greg? Tell me, is it by his age, job, finance, health or wealth?" KJ said with a soft-spoken voice. She paused. "Again I ask how do you know a grown man?"

"A grown man is someone who can handle his business."

"What about home?"

"That's a part of the business."

"I don't think so, Greg... you see, when a man gets confused with his office and his home, he's still a growing man. When a man refers to his wife, or significant other, as partner, he's still a growing man; when a man checks his finances every day, he's still a growing man; when a man calls his house a crib, he's still a growing man."

"The business is part of a growing man, KJ," Greg said, agitated.

"Don't get uptight, just listen. A house is just a house until you make it a home; home is where the heart is; there are no partners in a home, just a husband, wife and children, and the only crib is where the baby sleeps. The only finances you should be checking are the bills and mortgage being paid on time, and while you are growing you are preparing for the day you become a grown man. Are you listening, Greg?"

"I hear ya, KJ," Greg said, clearing his throat.

"But did you understand?"

"Yes, I did." Greg paused and looked at KJ, she smiled at him. "I guess..." He cleared his throat again. "I guess I'm still growing, huh KJ?"

"Don't worry, Greg, we've all got some kind of growing to do, we fail to realize that our age doesn't make us grown, that's just a number, and kids are lying about that every day, but it's what we achieve during those years that makes the difference."

"Amen to that," Greg said, laughing.

"You're crazy, you know that," KJ said, laughing with him.

They arrived at Emma's house. She lived on a very posh

street, and the homes were huge.

"Wow, you sure this is the right address?"

"Greg, I know you've been here before, so don't act like it's your first time."

"She told, huh?"

KJ nodded her head.

"Okay then." Greg unbuckled his seat belt, opened the car door, looked back at KJ and said, "She really told you?"

Greg was busted, but you can't blame a man for trying.

Aunt Lou opened the door. She looked over at the car and KJ waved, she waved back and went inside with Greg following her, he closed the door. It wasn't five minutes before both of them came walking toward the car.

Emma looked stunning with her black, knee-length sequined dress with a high neckline and low cut back, matching black, ankle strapped sequined shoes and a small black purse, her long hair left loose.

"You look every bit of twenty-one, Emm, happy birthday."

KJ handed Emma a long red box as she buckled her seat belt.

"What's this?"

"Open it and see."

Emma opened the box.

"Oh, my goodness, this is beautiful, KJ, when did you have time to get this?"

At that moment Greg coughed, seeking attention.

"Okay, Greg and I looked on-line; when we both saw the bracelet with twenty-one diamonds we knew it was the perfect gift, he went and picked it up for me."

"Thank you both."

"No baby, thank me, Greg just picked it up for me."

KJ glanced at Greg, raising her eyebrows. He turned the key in the ignition and started driving. Eventually Greg pulled up at a breathtaking hotel on the beach, and as they pulled in to valet park, they could smell the fresh sea air. The valet opened the car door and they stepped out, the valet giving Greg the ticket.

"This is some place," KJ said. "Is it new?"

"Fairly," Greg responded, as he walked around the car.

"Grab an arm, ladies," Greg said, looking at each of them. "I'll be the envy of every man here tonight."

KJ, Greg and Emma started laughing as they walked arm in arm through the lobby. They stopped in front of the elevator and Greg pressed the button.

"Why are we taking the elevator, aren't the restaurants usually on the ground floor?" asked Emma.

"What are you worrying about, this is *your* night, just relax, do you think I'd take you to a room with grandma?"

KJ nudged him and all three burst into hysterics.

When the elevator doors opened, it was as if stepping into a movie. Inside was like a wraparound flat screen television, from the center up, on all three walls except for the doors - it was amazing. Greg inserted a key into the slot provided and the elevator doors closed as a voice said, 'going up'. KJ and Emma were beside themselves. 'Rooftop restaurant', the elevator said, and then the doors opened.

"This is out of this world," KJ said, astonished, just looking around.

Emma was equally fascinated.

"Reservation for three under the name Greg Haven," Greg said to one of the uniformed staff.

"This way, Sir," said the man in black and white holding what seemed like a reservation book.

He pulled the chairs out for all three of them.

"Enjoy your meal, your waiter will be with you shortly."

The roof was like a glass dome, they could see the moon and stars, there was also a live band playing soft jazz in the background. This is so romantic, Emma thought as Greg ordered a bottle of champagne to celebrate the occasion.

"May I take your orders?"

"If the ladies are ready," Greg replied.

"Yes, I'll have the roast duck in orange sauce, with new potatoes and vegetables, please," ordered KJ.

Emma chose the grilled salmon with wild rice and steamed

broccoli, and Greg, the steak well done, with mashed potatoes and gravy, no vegetables.

"Thank you," said the waiter, and he walked away to place the orders.

Greg, KJ and Emma made small talk, listening to the music, going from one subject to another. Their food arrived and looked every bit delicious as their surroundings. Greg held their hands and blessed the food before they ate. KJ looked at him and smiled as though to say, 'I'm impressed'. The food was great, the three of them had a pleasant evening and not once did they mention MB Design. It was all about them as friends.

As they made their way back to the car, Greg stopped.

"I'll meet you both at the valet station."

"Okay."

KJ shrugged her shoulders. They both walked through the lobby, once again admiring the art décor.

"You ladies didn't get far. Here, this is for you, and these are for you."

Greg handed KJ a single red rose and Emma a dozen.

"Thank you both for a wonderful evening. Now, let me get you lovely ladies home; I have church in the morning."

Greg gave the valet attendant his ticket and he went for the car. The night air had gotten cold and it seemed like the valet was taking forever. Greg wore a short sleeved, chocolate-colored linen shirt and apologized that he didn't have a jacket to put over their shoulders. The valet arrived and they both couldn't have got into the car any faster. They arrived at Emma's house, she was feeling tired after drinking a glass of champagne.

"Good night, KJ, see you on Monday, thank you for being there."

Emma blew KJ a kiss as Greg walked her to the door.

Emma opened the door, Greg gave her a peck on the cheek and said good night, she thanked him again and went inside.

"Now, let's get you home, KJ."

There was no response; KJ had fallen asleep. I guess I'm going to have to entertain myself, Greg thought. He arrived at KJ's house feeling very unsafe. There were a few hoodlums on the street playing dice, and the music was real loud. He parked the car as close to KJ's house as possible, given there were no empty spaces near her door. He doubled parked the car and reached over in his seat to nudge his passenger.

"We're here, KJ."

"Oh my, that was fast, did I sleep all the way?"

"Yes, you did."

"Thank you, Greg, for a wonderful evening, drive home safely okay."

Greg walked KJ to her door, and made sure she was in safely, while all the time watching his car.

"I will, good night KJ, see you on Monday."

Seven

"Good morning, Pam," said Emma, sounding blissful.

"Well, good morning to you too, you're mighty happy this morning."

"I'm always happy," replied Emma.

"I see you've let your hair down too."

Pam looked at her, raising her eyebrows and giving her the 'um' look.

"I have. You know, I had such a wonderful weekend, and I'm now the legal age to enter into society," Emma said, mimicking the English accent and turning her nose up in the air.

"Well, let me give you the proper good morning."

Pam rushed from behind the reception counter and curtsied in front of Emma.

"Why… Thank you, Madam, you may rise," Emma said, again with an English accent.

Both Pam and Emma burst into laughter.

"Thank you for making my morning, Emm," Pam said, giving her a hug.

Emma walked toward the elevator, strutting her stuff from left to right, with Pam watching and laughing, not laughing at what she was doing, but because Greg was also watching. When she turned around after pressing the elevator button and saw Greg, she almost tripped on her heel.

"Don't stop on my account, I was enjoying the view," Greg said, smiling.

"Good morning to you, too, Mr. Haven."

"Mr. Haven..." Greg repeated.

Pam whispered in Greg's ear.

"She's English this morning."

"Okay," he answered, then walked toward the elevator. "I trust you had a pleasant weekend, Ms. Trent?" Greg said, also mimicking the English accent.

Emma looked over at Pam, suggesting she had told him about their little charade that morning. She coughed, trying to get Pam's attention.

"She's not looking," Greg said, looking at her reflection through the mirror.

The elevator came and both Emma and Greg stepped in.

"What's on your agenda this morning?" Greg asked, trying to make small talk.

"I have a meeting with Squares this morning," Emma answered.

"Do you mind if I sit in?"

Emma looked at Greg quizzically.

"Why would you want to sit in on this meeting?"

The elevator arrived on the eighth floor and Emma stepped out before Greg could give her an answer.

"I'll call you when I get to my office," Greg said before the doors closed.

"Okay," Emma responded, and continued toward her office.

As Emma approached her office door, she heard the second elevator doors open. She turned around to see who was exiting, and it was KJ.

"Good morning, Emm, how are you this morning?" KJ said in her motherly caring voice.

"I'm fine," Emma said, feeling not as perky as she had been when she first arrived that morning.

"Then why the long face?" asked KJ.

"Oh, it's..."

"Let me guess... Greg? When are you going to get it into your head that this man is head over heels for you?" KJ said, looking at Emma.

"It's not that," she said, continuing to walk to her office with KJ at her side.

"He wants to be in the meeting this morning with Squares."

"Why?" KJ said, confused, knitting her eyebrows.

"Your guess is as good as mine, but he said he'll call to explain."

Just then the phone rang. KJ looked at the display and gave

Emma the look.

"Talk about the Devil and he appears."

Emma smiled and walked to her desk while KJ answered the phone and transferred the call.

"Hello again," Emma said.

"Well, hello to you, too," said Greg, with his sexy deeper-than-usual voice.

"How can I help you?" Emma asked, trying to maintain her professionalism.

"Well, you can start by inviting me to your meeting this morning with Squares."

"Why are you interested in this meeting, Greg?"

"Well, they have a new line of men's clothing coming out, and I would like to get a glimpse before it hits the market."

"And that's the only reason?" Emma asked, feeling a little relieved.

"That's the only reason... besides looking at your beautiful face."

"I'll see you at the meeting, nine o'clock on the third floor."

"Okay."

Emma hung up the phone and just as she did so KJ walked in with the morning coffee.

"It's flavored this morning; a little chocolate, cinnamon and whipped cream."

"Is this a special Monday, or am I missing something?" Emma asked, giving KJ a guilty look.

"You tell me," KJ said, taking a sip of her coffee and looking at Emma over the rim of her coffee cup. "It's not every day handsome comes your way, don't shut the door until you've taken a look inside, it might surprise you, doors have a way of fooling people and sometimes people have a way of fooling doors, either way there's always something or someone behind them."

"What are you talking about?" Emma responded, acting like she didn't know what KJ was saying.

"I know you understand me, Emm... anyway, let me get back to business. I have a few thank you cards to send out to the crew, thanking them for a very successful first fashion show."

"Good idea, why didn't *I* think of that?"

"Because you told me to use my God-given talents and make us shine."

"Thank you, KJ, I really appreciate you."

"Ditto," KJ said, and walked back to her desk, closing the door to Emma's office behind her.

Pam called up to Emma's office to let her know that Squares were running a little late, maybe thirty minutes or so, which was great for Emma because she wanted to take a look at their portfolio to get herself familiarized with their line of fashion before the meeting.

Emma sat at her desk, but she suddenly jumped up and walked toward the window. There she is! Emma thought. She's like clockwork. Where does she live? Why is she here every day? Emma found herself asking these strange questions about a woman she didn't even know. She was so intrigued by her beauty and elegance, even from a distance she could see the grace and poise just from the way she sat on the bench.

"Watching that woman again I see," KJ said as she walked in.

"You startled me," Emma said, "I didn't hear you come in."

"You never do when you're looking at her, it's like she takes you to a different place," KJ said as she placed the day's mail on Emma's desk.

"Anything good?"

"Not really, mostly junk," KJ replied.

"May I come in or are you two ladies talking girl stuff?"

KJ turned around to face Greg with a smile on her face.

"Good morning to you, too."

"Didn't I say good morning to you when I called earlier?"

"Yes, you did, but that was via the phone, and now you're here in person, I expect another one."

"Well, top o' the morning to ya," Greg said, mocking the Irish accent.

"Whatever," KJ said as she walked past him to her desk.

Emma laughed and handed Greg the portfolio for Squares.

"What's this?"

"Oh, I'm sorry, it's Square's portfolio; I thought you might want to look at it before the meeting."

Greg looked at his watch, it was after nine.

"Shouldn't we get going?" he asked.

"They called, they're running thirty minutes late," Emma said, leaning back in her chair.

"Oh, so you just conveniently forgot to call me to tell me they were running late," Greg said as he pulled up a chair and sat across from Emma.

"Well… I was distracted."

"With what?" Greg asked, looking around her office.

Emma felt herself getting hot. She tilted her head back exposing her full neckline, closing her eyes she took her right hand, smoothing her neck from her throat up to her chin. Greg sat there mesmerized by her beauty; he couldn't contain himself any longer.

"Emma."

"Yes," she responded softly.

"What are you doing?" Greg said, trying to regain his composure.

"I'm rubbing my neck, what does it look like?"

"I'm sorry, for a moment I thought you were seducing me,"

Greg said, still staring at her.

Emma stopped, opened her eyes and looked at him.

"Tell me you didn't say what I thought you just said."

Greg backed up his chair and walked toward her.

"Oh, I said what you thought I said."

"Greg, what are you doing, you're getting a bit close, let go of my hand, I don't want to stand…"

There was silence. KJ sat outside the door, giving herself the 'about time' expression.

"Wow!" Emma exclaimed, shocked at what had just taken place.

"I waited a whole year for that, and it was worth every minute," Greg said, holding Emma close and removing the hair from her face.

"I don't know what to say."

Greg put his forefinger on her lips.

"You don't have to say anything. I'll check with Pam to see where we are with Squares, you just pull yourself together and I'll call you."

Greg stepped back and walked toward the door. Emma was still standing there in front of her chair. What just happened here? she thought. He kissed me, she was still in, huh? She tried to pull herself together, fearing KJ would walk through the doorway at any moment, but she didn't.

"Okay, we're on our way," said KJ, responding to Pam calling to let them know the representatives from Squares had just arrived and were making their way to the third floor conference room.

"Knock, knock," KJ said, pretending to knock on Emma's door, "the reps from Squares are here."

"Okay," Emma said, trying not to make eye contact with KJ.

"It's called love or something like that."

"What are you talking about now, KJ?" Emma said, spinning around her office looking for something;

"What are you looking for?" KJ said. "You're making me dizzy going back and forth… *stop*!"

KJ grabbed hold of Emma's arm.

"Take a deep breath, find your lipstick and pin your hair up, I'll go on ahead and let them know you're on your way."

KJ walked out of Emma's office and went on ahead of her to the meeting, while Emma composed herself. KJ pressed the elevator button and waited a few seconds until it arrived. When the doors slid open there stood Greg, looking past KJ for Emma.

"Where's Emma?"

"Oh, she's looking for her lipstick."

"Her lipstick," Greg repeated;

"Well, didn't you take it off, Mr. Look-so-Good?"

Greg laughed.

"She told you that?" he said, feeling embarrassed.

"No, she didn't have to, but take it one day at a time, okay Greg."

"I will. Thank you, KJ, you really are something, and I mean that," Greg replied sincerely.

Eight

"It's been almost five years, Emm, since you and Greg started dating. Has he ever talked about marriage?" KJ said, while she and Emma had their morning tea.

"No, never... sometimes I think he's hiding things from me, or maybe it's just me."

KJ was concerned.

"Why would you say that?"

"Well, he's has a lot of out of town meetings to go to, none of which are scheduled, he also has these *boys'* weekend trips, but I've never met any of the boys."

"So, what you're saying is, you think he's being dishonest?"

"Well, everything has been great with Greg over the past four years, our relationship couldn't be better, however, I'm still having problems in the bedroom and I'm not sure if that's what's causing him to have these weekends away."

"I would be too if I lived across the other side of town. What were you thinking when you backed out of the deal to buy the house together?" KJ asked, slightly agitated.

"I got scared, in a word..." Emma paused. "The funny thing is, when I told him I wasn't buying the house with him, he walked out and said nothing. When he came by the next evening,

I sensed something different about him, he couldn't look me in the eyes as he normally would when we talked, especially when we were close."

"Why would you be scared, and scared of whom? Greg?"

KJ looked at Emma and could see there was something clearly wrong with the picture.

"Okay, why don't we start from the beginning?" she said.

"The beginning," Emma repeated, and shrugged her shoulders.

She pushed her chair back from the desk and stood up. She moved her tea cup and placed it in the center of her desk as she walked toward the window.

"My first year in college," Emma began, "I wanted to be among the elite crowd, however, there was a price to pay, which I was not aware of. One Saturday night the girls and I went to a bar, and, prior to going, I heard a group of girls talking and giggling, unaware I was the subject. When we got to the bar I noticed there weren't many men there, maybe two were bartenders and a couple at the door, I didn't think anything of it. Anyway, about an hour after having a few drinks one of the girls, Kathy Rawlings, I'll never forget the name, said if I wanted to be among the elite crowd I had to do a dare. I thought they were joking, but they weren't laughing. I was asked to go in a room at the back of the bar with the red light flashing and wait for fifteen minutes then come out. I asked if that was it, and they said 'yes' and started laughing because I had had a few too many to drink. I didn't think anything of it at the time, but they were buying me drinks left, right and center, now I know why.

I went into the room with the flashing red light at the back of the bar and waited fifteen minutes. By that time the alcohol had consumed me, the ceiling starting revolving, I sat on the bed, laid back and closed my eyes hoping the alcohol would wear off, and fell asleep. The next morning I found myself naked, still on the bed with a man lying next to me, also naked. I jumped off the bed, got dressed and ran out of there. I couldn't scream I felt so dirty and deceived. As I approached the main bar, I was stopped by a woman, who said I was lucky she came when she did."

"Why, what happened?" KJ said, asking Emma to continue.

"She said if she hadn't come along when she did... my innocence would have been lost forever."

KJ let out a sigh of relief.

"I asked her who took my clothes off, she said she did, because the man had thrown up over me and himself, so she had to strip the two of us, but I hadn't felt a thing. She warned me about the danger of alcohol and 'friends'. Since that night I haven't touched a drop of alcohol, but I have nightmares of what could have happened, hence why I've never dated, I've been too scared."

"So, how does Greg make you feel?" Emma said, smiling.

"He has the softest hands, they're warm and gentle. The first time he touched me I felt safe, secure, when he whispered, 'I won't do anything until you're ready'. I almost melted in his arms, but he respected that, he gave me the most passionate kiss and said he had to leave."

"Leave, where were you?" KJ asked suspiciously, looking at Emma strangely.

"At my house," Emma said, trying not to laugh.

"With Aunt Lou!" KJ exclaimed, trying to imagine what Aunt Lou would have done if she had caught the two of them.

"Putting all jokes aside, KJ, I owe a lot to ZaNé."

"Who is ZaNé?"

"She's the lady who saved me. At the time she owned the bar. She said she saw when the girls sent me back there and knew exactly what they were up to, however, she must have been busy, or turned her back when drunk Pete came by. She came back there to see how I was doing, that's when she saw him leaning over me, throwing up, he collapsed on the bed, and the rest you know. She's since renovated the bar; she and her girlfriend turned it into a bistro and are joint owners."

"She and her girlfriend, you mean…"

"Yes, I mean… they are lesbians."

Emma stared at KJ, waiting to see her expression, but she

simply said:

"Do you keep in touch with her?"

"She's the reason why I thought I was confused. She's so in control, very concerned for the environment and talks a lot about helping young adults make the right decisions in life and being happy with whom they are."

"But you were so young then, merely eighteen," KJ said.

"I was intelligent, book smart, but didn't know anything about the streets and friends, I was so naïve," Emma said, getting angry with herself.

"Have you seen ZaNé since graduating?" KJ asked out of curiosity.

"Not since graduation night, when Aunt Lou and I had dinner at the bistro."

"You took Aunt Lou there, knowing how she feels about a woman's preferential choice in partners?"

"Yes, I did."

Emma walked back to her desk, sat in her chair and proceeded to tell KJ about the night of her graduation.

"This I've got to hear," said KJ.

Aunt Lou started drinking heavily when Emma left for college. She used to drink before, but not as much. When Emma was graduating from college six months early, Aunt Lou was so overjoyed she cried throughout the whole ceremony. After

Emma received her diplomas she walked around with Aunt Lou, congratulating her fellow graduates, stopping and taking pictures while walking toward the car. Partying was out of the question, especially after her first experience.

"We arrived at the bistro," Emma began, "it was packed, I heard someone say there was a one-hour waiting time. Aunt Lou looked at me over the rim of her glasses and folded her arms; I knew exactly what that meant. As we turned to head back to the car, I heard someone shout, 'Emma, Emma', and I looked back, it was ZaNé. 'Where you going?' she asked, catching up to us, sounding all puffed out of breath. I told her we were going home as it was so packed there, giving her the eye signal toward Aunt Lou. 'Oh,' ZaNé said, catching on, 'you don't have to worry about that, I saved you a table'.

I asked her how she knew I was coming, and we both burst out laughing, leaving Aunt Lou to her own imagination.

As we passed through the crowd I could feel the tension and looks we were getting as we made out way to the entrance door. 'Make way, please, for the graduate, special guest of mine', ZaNé said, all the while smiling. We finally reached the door and ZaNé showed us to our table, my special corner next to the window. 'See, I told you I saved you a table', ZaNé said as she walked away.

The waitress came over and gave me a hug and kissed me too

close to the mouth. Aunt Lou saw that and coughed into the tissue she held in her hand. The waitress, Cassi, CC for short, had no shame in her game. She was forty and preferred women also, was well educated, had a doctorate in sociology, but preferred to socialize instead. She and ZaNé had been business and personal partners for over twenty years, they named the bistro after converting it from a bar, WPL? with a question mark at the end-"

"What does WPL stand for?" KJ interrupted.

"When I first saw it two years ago after the renovation, I asked the same question. They both looked at each other and laughed. After a while ZaNé said, 'Women Preferred Ladies?', that's when they told me more about their lifestyle and partnership. They mentioned that women should not be afraid to express their feelings about who they are, but live life to the fullest, there are more important things in the world to be concerned about. Both had always respected who I was, although I really didn't know myself until the night of my graduation when CC went a bit too close to my mouth in front of Aunt Lou. I knew that wasn't the lifestyle for me, but I still wasn't sure, all I knew at that time was I was educated and unemployed."

"So, why the question mark?" KJ asked, looking at Emma with knitted eyebrows.

"Well, I'll tell you like they told me - do women prefer ladies?"

"Are you asking me?"

"Yes, I'm asking you," Emma responded.

"I don't know."

"Precisely," Emma said, leaving KJ a little confused.

"Anyway," she continued, "I started a conversation with Aunt Lou...

'How was your steak, Aunty?' 'Okay, I guess' she replied, looking down at the plate, moving the meat from one side to the other. 'So, why didn't you eat it?' I asked, a little upset. 'Don't take that tone with me, Emma Trent, I guess I wasn't that hungry after all.' 'Well, you'd better eat something; we have a three-hour drive back home'.

She looked at me over the rim of her glasses then looked over at ZaNé and CC, who were busy doing their greeting and socializing, paying no attention to our table at all. I saw where she was going and chose to ignore it.

'Are you?' she began, then she stopped. 'Are you what? Say it, Aunty,' I snapped. 'Am I what?' 'Are you like that?' 'Why? Would you love me less if I was?'

My tone was sharp and I could feel my temper rising, so I chose to quit the subject and talk about something else.

'So, now that I've graduated, are you going to tell me this big secret you've been keeping from me forever; who paid for my four-year college education, books and board?' Aunty Lou said it was a scholarship, but she couldn't remember the sponsors' names. 'I'd like to send them a thank you card', I continued, hoping to get something out of her, but Aunt Lou kept saying they knew I was grateful.

'You are so difficult, Aunt Lou.' I took a fifty dollar bill from my purse and placed it under the salt and pepper shaker, removed the napkin from my lap, got up and walked out of the bistro. I waved to ZaNé and CC, who were still busy. Aunt Lou followed, she never waved, although both ZaNé and CC shouted, 'It was nice meeting you, don't be strangers'.

We walked to the car in silence; neither of us said a word as we drove home."

"For three hours," KJ said.

"We stopped for gas and she said she had to use the bathroom, but that was it."

Just as KJ was settling down to hear more about Aunt Lou, the phone rang on Emma's private line.

"Would you like me to answer it?" KJ asked.

"Please," Emma replied.

"Hi, Greg, how are you?" said KJ. "Hold on, I'll give Emma the phone."

"Hi baby."

KJ walked out of the office laughing while Emma attempted to throw a pencil at her jokingly.

"I'm between meetings and I just wanted to hear that sexy voice of yours, what are you doing tonight?"

"I have nothing planned."

"Good, don't make any, I have a surprise for you, have to go, the next meeting's getting started, love you, baby."

He then hung up the phone. Emma was still holding the phone, staring into space...

"KJ, come here, please," Emma called, all excited.

"Yes, what is it, why are you shaking and still holding the phone?"

KJ took the phone from Emma's hand and placed it on the receiver.

"Greg just told me he loved me."

"Okay, before we have a heart attack here, what did he actually say?"

"He said not to make plans for tonight, he had a surprise for me, and before he hung up he said, 'love you, baby', do you think he's going to... well... you know?"

"No, I don't know what you are trying to propose," KJ said.

"That's it... *propose*, do you think he's g-going to pr-propose?" Emma said, stuttering and acting like a schoolgirl.

"Well, I sure hope so..." said KJ, and she walked out of the office.

*

Greg's meeting finished earlier than expected. When he arrived back in his office he called Emma, however, KJ told him she had just left to view some sample materials that had just been delivered from Squares. He asked that she return his call as soon as she got back in the office.

It was two days before Emma's twenty-sixth birthday. Greg sat at his desk wondering where the time had gone, and he reminisced back to the first time he had taken Emma and KJ out for dinner after their first fashion show, it had also been Emma's twenty-first birthday. He took a deep breath and sighed with disbelief that he'd been dating Emma for almost five years. He thought how she had matured over the years and she was very successful; she had put MB Design on a different level single-handedly, with her own design label, 'Elegant'. She had sure proved them wrong, all those who had doubted this twenty-year-old university graduate.

Greg took a red velvet box from his pocket and placed it on the desk in front of him. He stared at it for a moment before he picked it up and held it in the palm of his hand. He opened it and looked at the beautiful, 1.75 carat, hint of pink, radiant cut-diamond ring on a platinum mount he had just purchased for Emma. He was hoping to propose to her because he was so sure he was going to get the promotion for vice president that had been announced earlier in the week. Conner had advised all senior partners to apply, and because he had longevity and designee to Conner, he assumed the position was his for the taking, but due to company policy and formality they had to give each partner the opportunity to apply.

Greg closed the box and put it back into his pocket. He placed a call to Emma's office again, and this time KJ told him she had been called to Conner's office. He wondered what was going on, but kept his composure. He waited patiently for Emma to return his call.

Emma returned Greg's calls when she returned from her meeting with Conner.

"Hey, baby, KJ told me you called me twice, is everything okay?"

"Everything is fine now that I've heard your voice," said Greg.

"It's almost five o'clock, what time are you leaving the office?" asked Emma.

"In a few."

"Okay, whatever a few is…"

"I'll be leaving in five minutes; does that answer your question?"

"Yes, it does."

"Can you meet me at the house?"

"I don't have a key, remember."

"Did you check your mailbox today?"

"No, I didn't."

"Well, maybe you should."

"Okay, hold just for a minute."

Emma walked out to KJ's area and asked her if she had cleared the mailbox. She told her to look in the incoming tray on her desk.

"Nice red envelope."

"So, you did get it," Greg said, with his deep masculine voice. "Did you open it?"

"I don't need to; I can feel what it is."

"Okay, I'll meet you at the house. Call Aunt Lou so she won't worry about you."

"I'll stop home first just to make sure she's all right."

"That sounds great. I'll see you back at the house."

Greg hung up the phone. Emma gathered her things and walked out of her office. She waited for KJ to grab her purse and jacket then they both left together.

"So, what are you doing for the weekend?" asked KJ.

"I'm going to Greg's this evening, and then maybe to the mall tomorrow, I haven't been there in a while. Why, what are you doing?"

"The girls and I are going shopping and maybe take in a movie; it's mother and daughters' weekend, I promised them."

"That is so lovely, KJ, enjoy them while you can."

"I know that's right," KJ replied.

They exited the elevator and parted. As Emma was walking toward her car, she noticed the lady on the bench. She smiled at her, got up and walked away, her white shawl blowing in the light evening air. Emma stood there and watched her walk away from the building. She has such an elegant walk, she thought, but why does she spend most of her days sitting on the bench? Emma shook her head and continued to walk to her car.

Just then she saw Greg leaving the building with Yaz. She didn't think anything of it until Yaz got into his car. Okay, what is going on? Emma thought. Let me take a deep breath and not act stupidly. She put the key in the ignition and drove off, looking back through her rear-view mirror at the two of them in his car. He pulled out and went the opposite way. Emma was imagining all sorts of things.

When she arrived home, she quickly checked in on Aunt Lou, packed a weekend bag then left. As she approached Greg's house, she saw his car parked in the driveway. She took yet another deep breath, thinking Yaz might be inside. She pulled up behind his shiny black BMW and parked her silver Honda. As she opened her car door, Greg came out to meet her, and she couldn't get out the car fast enough. He grabbed her and pulled her close to him.

"I've been waiting all day for this," he said, and gave her a long passionate kiss.

"I saw you leaving the office with Yaz, is she here?" Emma said, sounding upset.

"Well, I've been waiting all day for this too, honey," Greg said sarcastically. "What's with you, Emma, do you think I'd cheat with another woman right under your nose?"

Greg pulled away and started to walk back into the house. Emma closed the car door, got her bag and walked behind him.

"I'm sorry," she said as she entered the house.

"Don't worry about it… If you must know, I took Yaz to pick up her car; she just had it serviced at the dealers. She said she called you, but you had already left."

"I thought I heard the phone when I was leaving, but KJ and I had already locked up."

Emma walked toward the bedroom to put her bags down. She could tell Greg was still a little upset by the tone of his voice, so she knew she had to make it up to him. She put the bags in the room and went out into the lounge.

"Would you like a drink?" he asked.

"Yes, a brandy, please."

Greg looked at her in astonishment.

"A brandy," he repeated.

"Yes, please," said Emma shyly, thinking that she needed

something to relax her and wake her up.

"Okay, a brandy it is, how would you like it?"

"On the rocks with a sprig of mint."

"One brandy on the rocks with a sprig of mint coming up, make yourself comfortable."

Emma went and sat on the big overstuffed, red suede sofa, in front of the smokeless imitation fire. Greg had built the fireplace especially for that wall, it was so cozy. There was no television in that area, he called it the 'winding down' room. There was a large white rug in the center with a smoked class coffee table, and identical loveseats to the left and right, also overstuffed red suede. To either side of the sofa were smoked glass end tables with tiffany lamps on each. To the right side of the fireplace he had a set of fireplace utensils and to the left, a rack containing his CD collection. The stereo he had mounted into a smoked glass case with surround sound and it was operated by remote control. The place was fabulous, the man had exquisite taste.

"Here's your drink," said Greg. "Would you like to listen to some music?"

"That would be nice."

"You know... you don't have to be a stranger when you come here. Even though you walked out on the deal, I still consider this your home too, so relax, and take your shoes off."

Emma took a sip of her drink and immediately felt the effect.

She took her shoes off and curled up on the sofa, looking at a magazine. Greg came over to her, took the magazine out of her hand and began to kiss her...

"Now, let's start this evening over again, shall we?" Greg said, staring into her eyes.

"Okay, let's," Emma said, putting her arms around his neck.

They greeted each other again then they both started laughing. Emma took another sip of her drink and told Greg she was going to take a shower. Greg put on some light jazz and dimmed the lights down, creating the mood for him to propose. He felt his jacket pocket to make sure the box was still there, he smiled and went into the bedroom. He could hear the shower and was tempted to join her, but instead chose to use the guest bathroom.

When Emma came out of the shower, she oiled her skin with white musk, a mild sensual fragrance, put on her black thong with a long, black lace nightgown and pinned her hair up into a French twist. As she left the bedroom she could hear Greg singing in the next shower. She went back into the lounge and lay down on the sofa. She picked up her glass from the coffee table, took a sip and placed it on the end table. She heard the shower stop, and her heart started racing. She felt different, although she and Greg had been dating, this night felt different, she felt free as though she had nothing to hide anymore, all the tension gone.

When Emma heard Greg approaching the lounge, she sat up in the sofa, looked over the top and watched as he walked toward her, his well-oiled six-pack and biceps just shining in the dimly lit room. She marveled at his tall physique and well-toned legs, masculine hands, not to mention the silk boxer shorts, for she had forgotten what an all-round handsome man Greg was without his suit on.

"Do you mind if I sit next to you?" Greg said, just looking at Emma, shaking his head.

She held out her hand and guided him to sit to the left of her. He looked at her intently.

"There's something different about you tonight, Emm, I can't put my finger on it, but I like it."

Emma had the brandy glass in her hand, almost empty.

"Would you like another drink?"

"Okay," she said, feeling warm inside.

"Are you sure you can handle it?" Greg asked, concerned.

"Don't worry about what I can handle," Emma whispered.

"*Did you say something?*" Greg yelled.

"No," Emma responded.

Just hurry back, she thought. She watched him as he went to the bar area of the house and poured them both a drink. He came back and sat beside her again. She took a sip of her drink, placed the glass on the side table and leaned back into the sofa, putting her feet on Greg's lap. He put both her feet on the sofa and knelt down on the floor facing her. He put his hand in his drink and took out a piece of ice, which he placed between her breasts on the neckline of her nightgown. She closed her eyes as, with his ice-cold fingertips, he began to gently touch her nipples. She could feel her heart beating uncontrollably as he proceeded to gently kiss her lips, moving down to her breast, placing his fingertips in her mouth.

As he moved down to the lower part of her body and removed her thong, he took hold of her hand and guided her to the white rug on the floor in front of the cozy lit fire. He removed her nightgown and lay her down. He took another piece of ice, this time rubbing it against both her nipples, making them hard. He took a sip of his drink and fed her mouth to mouth.

Emma rolled over and removed his boxer shorts, exposing his well risen penis, thanking whomever for giving him a double portion. She put her legs over him as he lay on the rug. She reached for her glass and took a mouthful of drink, drizzling it from her mouth down his body. She placed her mouth over his organ and released the last drop of drink, then worked her way back up his body. He held her, rolled her over and began to make passionate love to her. He ran his hand down her arched back and pulled her toward him. Sweat was pouring off the two of them. He turned her over and leaned her against the red loveseats, continuing from a different position.

"I've never seen you like this..." Greg whispered, holding her from the back.

"I don't want to talk..." she said, taking the clip from her hair. "Just hold me."

"Okay, baby..."

"Can you do it little harder?"

"Like this?"

Greg held her tighter.

"Harder, harder, Greg!" she screamed as she came to her climax.

Greg gave her all he had then he too reached his pinnacle point. They both fell to the floor and looked up at the ceiling.

"Whatever it is, I'll buy all of it," said Greg.

"What are you talking about?" Emma asked, feeling flushed.

"I don't know, you tell me," Greg said.

He turned toward her, leaning on his elbow with his hand holding his head, touching her nipple with his other hand.

"So, are you going to tell me what's going on, where all this sudden passion is coming from?"

Emma looked up at him, shook her head and smiled.

"I've been with you now, what, five years, almost five years? We've made love several times and I've never felt loved. Today you called and told me you loved me and made me feel special, like we had something meaningful. You've never said those three words before, that's one of the reasons why I'm not living here with you permanently. I've waited patiently for you to say it, although you've shown it in many ways, I wanted to *hear* it."

"If I had known this back then, I would have said it a long time ago. I have never seen you reach your peak, and damn, it felt good, so good, I'm ready for the second round."

"Oh no, baby, this lady needs her beauty sleep, how about round two for breakfast, with your new vice president?"

"Excuse me…" Greg said, removing his hand from her body.

"Your new vice president. Conner called me into his office today and offered me the position. He will be making the announcement on Monday."

Greg got up from the floor and put his boxer shorts on. Before going to the bar for another drink, he went into the master bedroom and picked up the box, which he had placed on her side of the bed, opened it, looked at the ring, slammed it shut and put it into his closet behind a stack of books on the top shelf. He felt so betrayed. Emma hadn't noticed the look on Greg's face, thinking he would be happy for her.

"Greg, what are you doing?"

"I'll be there in a minute," he replied.

Emma heard the shower. She got up from the floor, put her nightgown on and went to meet Greg in the bedroom. As she approached the door, she saw him coming out of the shower, but instead of getting into bed he got dressed in a sweat suit and put his sneakers on.

"Where are you going?"

"To get some Chinese, I'm hungry."

"Why don't you order it? They deliver," said Emma, feeling a little tipsy.

"Yeah, I know, but I need some fresh air," Greg replied with a sigh.

"Did I do something wrong, Greg?"

"On the contrary, you did everything right."

"May I come with you then?"

"Baby, I'll be right back."

He gave her a kiss on the forehead, grabbed her car keys and left.

Nine

The alarm went off at 5:30 A.M. Emma jumped from a deep sleep, reaching for the clock to turn the alarm off. She reached for the wrong side of the bed, and suddenly realized she was still at Greg's. She stretched over the untouched side of the bed and turned the alarm off. She threw the sheets back, rolled out of the bed, took one step then put her hands to her head...

I have the worse headache, she thought to herself. She stepped back, sat on the edge of the bed and called out for Greg. There was no answer, so she called again - still no answer. She got up then sat down again, took a deep breath then got up and staggered to the door. She went through the house and still no sign of Greg, she looked out of the window and her car was nowhere in sight.

Emma went back into the bedroom and reached for the phone. She called Greg's cell phone. There was no answer, but the machine picked up, she left no message. She held the phone in her hand then hung it up. She was tempted to call again, but she didn't, instead she took a cold shower and got dressed in blue jeans and a white shirt, with white ankle strap sandals.

Emma knew Greg kept a spare set of keys to his car in a toolbox in the garage, so she went looking for the keys in the usual place, but they were not there. She searched high and low, and still no sign of the keys, then she stumbled upon another toolbox in the corner of the garage, covered with a neatly folded burgundy, oversized beach towel. Emma moved the towel and noticed the box had a padlock on it. She picked the box up, thinking it was rather light for tools. Curious, Emma frantically looked for something to open the lock. She searched through the other toolbox and found a pair of pliers. She tried and tried until she finally broke the lock.

Emma took her hand and threw the hair from her face, sweating with her heart racing. She sat down on the garage floor and lifted the lid of the box. She took out the first envelope and recognized the handwriting - it was Yaz's. Why would Yaz's letters be here? Emma's heart started beating faster as she read through the letters, and then she found a sealed envelope from an out-of-state court, addressed to Mr. and Mrs. Haven.

Greg's married? she thought. She got up from the floor and rushed to Greg's computer to search for the court. To her surprise it was still on; he had been in the middle of drafting an E-mail that read:

To Yazzie,

Sorry about the weekend, but Emma will be here, you understand, I've got to do this. I have to put closure to this relationship once and for all, we're married now and I know we've had our ups and downs, but Jayden is our son and I cannot go through with the divorce.

I need you in my life, Yaz, please forgive me for all I have put you through. Anyway, the check is in the usual place, drive safely and give Jayden a big hug from da…

Emma read it twice and began to cry uncontrollably. She picked up the phone and called KJ.

KJ answered the phone still half-asleep.

"Hello, who is this? Slow down, I can't understand a word you're saying. Emma, is that you?"

"Greg's cheating with Yaz," Emma said, screaming on the phone, she didn't have the nerve to mention he was married.

"Slow down, where are you?"

"I'm at Greg's house," she said, sniveling.

"Okay, that's not too far, I'll catch a cab. I'll be there in thirty minutes or so, by the way, where is Greg?" KJ asked.

"I don't know, he left last night, said he was going for Chinese, I haven't seen or heard from him since, he took my car. I was looking for the spare keys to his car so I could leave, that's when I found the box-"

KJ interrupted.

"Tell me when I get there, I won't be long, don't do anything stupid, okay?"

Emma hung up the phone, lay on the bed and cried. She suddenly remembered the padlock and quickly speed dialed KJ's number.

"Hello."

"It's me again. I found her letters and an envelope from an out-of-state court. I went to the computer to look up the public records for that state. He was composing an E-mail to her, I must have interrupted him and he forgot to send it... Why would he do this to me, KJ?"

"Well, maybe you're reading too much into it!" KJ said, trying to be sympathetic.

"KJ, I know what I read, he said something about they also have a son, Jayden."

"A son," KJ repeated, "this is serious. I'll be there as soon as I can."

Emma hung up the phone, went back into the garage and tried to put the letters back into the box as she had found them. The box slipped from her hand and all the contents fell to the ground. As she picked them up, she noticed an open Mercedes envelope. She read the contents; it was the title for a red Mercedes Benz, but Greg drove a black BMW. She continued reading. The title was for Yazmyne Haven. She pulled herself together, went back into the bedroom and called KJ again.

"KJ, before you get here, please stop at that 24-hour

hardware store and pick up a padlock. Here's the number, it has to be exact, hurry, I don't know when he'll be back."

"Okay, I'm on my way."

"Hurry."

"Okay."

Emma went back into the garage and put all the contents back into the box then waited near the front door, looking out of the window for KJ. It seemed like she took forever to get there. When the yellow cab pulled up outside the house, Emma opened the door and ran outside to meet KJ.

"You look a mess, girl; get back inside before the neighbors start talking," KJ said.

"I know. Did you get the right lock?" Emma said, panicking.

"I hope so."

"Let me see."

"Here…"said KJ, handing Emma the padlock.

"Perfect," Emma said. "Let's go into the garage."

Emma showed KJ where the box was, and asked her to help straighten things up. As they were putting things back, Emma went to freshen up in the bedroom before Greg returned; she didn't want him asking too many questions. KJ stayed in the garage putting things away. She lifted what she thought were old newspapers, but in fact they were covering up photo albums. She picked up one of the albums and started flipping through it.

There they were - wedding pictures of Yaz and Greg. She looked closer at the group pictures and thought she was seeing things, but as she turned more pages, as clear as day, Yaz, Greg and *Pam*. KJ closed the album and put it back where she found it before Emma came back. She wouldn't mention it to Emma. Just then Emma came back into the garage, startling KJ.

"I didn't hear you coming," KJ said, carefully looking at the floor, making sure the albums were covered.

"You know, he always said he never used this garage because the door was unpredictable. He said it had a faulty joint. My thing is, KJ," Emma continued, "why did he want me to buy this house with him if he's married to Yaz?"

"I don't know, Emm, but I'd like to get out of here, if you don't mind."

KJ felt as though she was invading Greg's privacy.

"Yes, of course, I'm sorry."

Emma offered KJ a cup of coffee to try and make things look as normal as possible for when Greg showed up.

"Yes, please."

"Well, I can tell you this… I gave him the greatest send-off last night," said Emma, striking up a conversation with KJ as she walked around the table to put the water to boil for the coffee.

"What do you mean send-off?" KJ said, losing Emma in conversation.

"You know, I gave him the time of his life, to celebrate my promotion."

"What promotion?"

"Conner offered me the vice president position; he'll make a formal announcement on Monday."

"That's fantastic, Emm, did you tell Greg?"

"Yes, I did, after the passion was over, I didn't want to spoil my fun. You know, KJ, I'm going places, just like Ms. Rose said I would be. I don't need to hang on to a married man, I've got a business to run."

"That's the spirit, Emm."

Just then they heard the key in the door - Greg was home. Emma played the worried girlfriend so well, with tears and all. If Oscars were awarded, she would have won for that scene, thought KJ, rolling her eyes away from the two of them.

"I thought something had happened to you, so I called KJ in case the police or hospital called. I couldn't bear to hear bad news on my own."

She threw her arms around him pretending to sob, and wiping her tears on his sweat suit. She stepped back and asked KJ if the water was hot for that cup of coffee she was about to make, to calm herself down.

"Yes, the water is ready," KJ said, playing her game.

"You go and sit down, KJ, I'll make the two of you some

flavored coffee. Is hazelnut and whipped cream okay, with a hint of cinnamon, chocolate and vanilla?" said Greg, as though nothing had happened.

"Sounds divine," KJ said, laughing, trying to get the images of the wedding photos out of her head while looking at Greg.

Emma looked over at KJ and mimed 'thank you'. KJ mimed back 'you owe me, big time'.

Greg made the coffees and then sat with Emma and KJ. He apologized to Emma for not coming home last night, saying he needed to clear his head.

"Is that what a wild night of passion does to a man?" Emma said, looking at him over the rim of her cup. "What are we going to do when we're married?"

"*Married*," Greg repeated.

"Yes, marriage, why not? We've been together now for, what, five years? I think we know each other very well for living apart. Although you've had a lot of business trips and working weekends away, I've had no reason not to trust you, so why not marriage?" Emma said, playing his game.

Greg looked at Emma and then put his head down.

"I'm not ready for marriage, Emma, not to you, anyway, not now, with the promotion, you're going to be swamped, and the last thing you need is to be planning a wedding."

"That's what I'm here for," said KJ, inviting herself into the conversation.

"Not you too!" Greg stood up and looked at Emma then at KJ. "I don't want to hear anything more about marriage, Emma, or from you, KJ, I'm serious, I'm not ready to marry you."

"Then when?"

"When I'm a millionaire?" he said as he walked toward the bedroom.

"I won't need you then, Greg, *I won't...*" Emma shouted after him.

He gave Emma such a look and continued to walk out of the lounge into the bedroom. Emma heard the water running, and went into the bedroom to make sure he was in the shower. She ran into his office and turned the computer off not to arouse any suspicion. She went back into the bedroom and shouted to him in the shower that she was leaving - he didn't respond.

"Let's go, KJ," Emma said, "I've had enough embarrassment for one Saturday morning. God knows, I don't need another thing to go wrong."

"Okay, you're the driver. Here; let me help you with those bags," said KJ as she helped Emma put the bags into the back of her car.

Emma opened the car door and sat in the driver's seat. As she put the key into the ignition, she saw Greg had left his phone in the car. KJ looked at her then at the phone.

"Take it inside, Emm, you're bigger than that," KJ said, knowing exactly what Emma wanted to do.

"He has two missed calls, who do you think the other call's from?"

"I don't know and I don't care," KJ answered, staring Emma in the eyes. "I'll take it in for you if you like."

"No, that's okay, like you said, I'm bigger than that."

Emma got out of the car holding the phone, still curious as to who had called. As she walked toward the door, the phone rang. She looked over at KJ gesturing 'what should I do?'. She looked at the caller ID, saw it was Yaz and she couldn't help herself. Emma flipped the phone open and put it to her ear.

"Hello, you, can you speak?" Yaz said in a sexy voice.

There was no response.

"Hello, hello," she said.

Emma closed the phone without saying a word, although tempted. She used the spare key to open the door, placed the phone on the counter close to the front door and walked out. As she did so, she heard the phone ringing again. Emma closed the door and walked toward the car.

"It was her," Emma said, frustrated as she sat in the car.

"Well, she *is* his wife, Emma, and you have to accept that, just move on with your life," KJ encouraged.

"I will move on with my life, KJ, just as soon as I find out what kind of game I'm playing and what are the rules, they forgot to give me instructions," she said as she put the car in reverse and drove out of the driveway.

"Take it easy, Emm, there are two lives in this car, slow down."

"I'm sorry, KJ, I didn't mean to alarm you."

Ten

"Good morning, Pam," KJ said, giving her an unfamiliar look.

"What did I do to deserve that look?" Pam said, with a curious look on her face.

"How about we have a talk, woman to woman?" said KJ, serious as a judge.

"What is this about, it's highly unusual for you to be here so early on a Monday morning, what's on your mind?" Pam said, concerned.

"I'm not going to beat around the bush with you, P-"

"I hoped you wouldn't," Pam interrupted, before KJ could finish her sentence.

"How long have Yaz and Greg been married?"

"Who told you they were married?" Pam said as she started straightening up papers behind the counter, avoiding eye contact with KJ.

"Will you stop doing that, and answer the question," KJ said, tense. "I saw the photos, Pam, Emma doesn't know, how you could string her on like that knowing she liked Greg and all this time he's married to Yaz."

"First of all, KJ, this is none of your business. If Miss Elegant wants to make a fool of herself then let her go right on doing it. Yaz has always been there for Greg through good times and bad. When she got pregnant it seemed like the right thing to do, when she took a leave last year, that's when it all happened. Her mother takes care of their son." Pam paused as tears filled her eyes. "Listen, KJ," she said in a soft voice. "Jayden, that's his name, he's a very sick child and I don't want any of this getting out, I've said too much already. It's only been a year. When Emma and Greg had that fight about the house, he went to Yaz for comfort and that's when they went a little too far, but to be honest with you, he has and will never stop loving Yaz."

"What's wrong with Jayden?"

"He has a rare blood disease. He's lived longer than the doctors expected," explained Pam.

"So, the unexplained meetings Greg's been attending are to see Jayden?"

"Yes."

Pam took the compact mirror from her purse, wiped the tears from her eyes and reapplied her smeared make-up with a fine brush.

"I don't understand why you would play this game with them, what are you getting out of this?"

"I'd rather not say anymore, KJ, I've really said enough."

KJ looked Pam in the eyes.

"You haven't heard the last of this, Pam," KJ said as she walked toward the elevator.

She pressed the elevator button just as Emma came waltzing through the doors.

"Good morning, Pam, how was your weekend?"

"Not bad," Pam replied, looking over at KJ.

"KJ, hold the elevator, please," Emma yelled. "See you later, Pam," she said as she rushed toward the elevator.

"Okay, Miss Emma," Pam said as she watched her rush toward KJ.

Emma handed KJ a small gift bag.

"I'm sorry to have spoiled your Saturday, KJ, so here."

"What is this, and when did you have time to go shopping?" KJ asked, surprised.

"After I dropped you off, I went home, had a good conversation with Aunt Lou and then went to the mall."

"Good on you, I was worried for a moment, I thought you were going to do something stupid."

"I did, I went shopping and spent lots of money, is that stupid enough?"

They arrived on the eighth floor. Emma took the keys out of her purse and opened the double glass doors. KJ went to her desk and Emma continued through the double doors to her office. The red light was on her phone, which meant she had messages, so she sat down to retrieve them - one was from Yaz.

"Hi, Emma, I guess I missed you, I wanted you to take me to pick up my car from the dealers, never mind, I'll call Greg before he leaves, have a great weekend."

End of messages. Emma gritted her teeth, stood up and walked toward the window.

"Emma, Pam is on the line for you," KJ said, not sounding her usual self.

Before Emma picked up the phone she asked KJ if everything was all right, she didn't answer. Emma picked up the phone.

"Pam, can I call you back?" Emma said, concerned about KJ. She placed the phone on the receiver and walked out to KJ's desk.

"What's with the voice?" Emma asked, standing in front of KJ, her arms folded.

"What voice?"

"That sad tone you use when something just isn't right."

"Everything is fine, Emm, really."

"Tell that to someone who doesn't know you," Emma said, and walked back into her office, still concerned about her assistant.   She sat at her desk, picked up the phone and returned Pam's call.

"Hey, Pam, how can I help you?"

"You sound like someone just died," said Pam.

"No, it's..."

KJ started waving to get Emma's attention, shaking her head. Emma could not understand, and asked Pam to hold on a moment.

"What is it, KJ?" Emma asked, knitting her eyebrows.

"I'm sorry, Emm, hang up with Pam, I need to talk to you." Emma released the hold button.

"Pam, I'll call you right back."

Before she could hang up the phone, Pam spoke.

"No, don't hang up again, listen, Conner wants to meet with you all at 8:00 A. M. in the large conference room on the ninth floor, he would also like KJ to be present."

"Okay, great, thank you. Pam, has Greg come in yet?"

"Why are you asking me for Greg?" Pam said, a little suspicious.

"No reason, I just wondered if he came in yet."

"No, I haven't seen him yet, well, speak of the devil, he just walked in. Do you need to speak to him?"

"Not right now, I'm meeting with KJ at the moment."

"With KJ?"

Again Pam sounded very suspicious.

"She *is* my assistant, Pam, remember?"

Emma hung up the phone and asked KJ to close the doors

and take a seat.

"What is on your mind, KJ?" Emma said, giving her a troubled look.

"I feel embarrassed to tell you this but…"

"But what?" Emma said.

"It's about Saturday."

"What about Saturday, KJ?"

Emma was now getting agitated. KJ paused.

"What about Saturday, KJ?" Emma repeated.

"Well, I'm not sure how to say this."

KJ couldn't figure out why she found it so difficult to tell Emma that Pam knew about the wedding, not only did she know, she attended.

"Why don't you just say it?" Emma said, trying to keep calm.

"Pam knew about the wedding, she also attended… there, I said it."

KJ couldn't have gotten the words out faster.

"What, I heard, wedding and Pam, what does Pam have to do with Saturday?" Emma said, looking confused.

"Pam attended the wedding, Emm," KJ said, looking down at her hands.

"How do you know this?" Emma said, staring KJ in the face.

"I stumbled across some photos in the garage at Greg's."

"How? I was with you the whole time."

"When you went to take care of something in the other room, I moved a stack of newspapers on the floor, the album was beneath them. I picked it up and looked at a couple of photos, and saw Pam as clear as day."

"And you thought not to tell me," Emma said, feeling a little betrayed.

"I didn't know whether or not you had seen them, so I didn't mention it." She felt so bad and could see the look on Emma's face.

"Sorry, Emm, I didn't want to upset you more than you already were."

"It's not your fault, KJ, I'm just a little confused at the moment. I'm not sure what's going on, but I'm going to find out one way or the other, and I'm going to need your help to do it, anyway I'm glad you told me. Let's get ready for this meeting."

"You mean, *you* get ready for *your* meeting."

"No, I mean *we*. Conner would like you to attend this one also."

KJ pushed her chair back, stood up, walked toward Emma and gave her a hug.

"How do I look, KJ?"

"Like a million dollar vice president."

Emma laughed as she and KJ walked through the doors heading for the elevator to the ninth floor.

The elevator doors opened on the ninth floor, there were balloons everywhere. As they approached the conference room and opened the door, Conner had a continental breakfast catered for the meeting, and each senior partner was there with their assistant.

"Please, everyone grab a plate and take a seat," was how Conner started the meeting. "As you all know, we have created a vice president position to take some of the load away from me. Production has been fantastic and from your bonuses I know we want to keep it that way, and with the addition of 'Elegant' clothing line created by Emma Trent, our magazine profits and new garment line have tripled over the past two years and are still rising. I have read each one of your applications carefully and made a decision based on production and how you have grown within the company. It was a hard decision to make because you have all done so well within your categories, but I'm not going to keep you all in suspense any longer, I would like to introduce to you the new vice president of MB Design, Ms. Emma Trent."

Most around the table clapped, whistled and cheered, except for Naomi, Greg and Yaz; they each looked at each other and gave a fake smile as Emma looked at them. Conner extended his hand and asked Emma to join him at the head of the table.

"I want you to get the feel of this chair. From now on you will be conducting the monthly meetings and overseeing all productions. You may promote from within or hire from outside, a suitable predecessor to fill your shoes as marketing director."

Emma looked over at KJ. She knew she could handle the job with her eyes closed, as they had created 'Elegant' together, however, she didn't want to put her on the spot, and decided to talk to Conner later with her decision.

Emma went back and sat with KJ and finished her breakfast. She looked up and saw Greg staring at her, and she glanced over at Yaz and gave her a smile. While sitting there KJ noticed the ring on Yaz's left hand and nudged Emma, giving her the eye signal. Emma looked over and saw the ring.

"That's a nice ring you have there, Yaz, I didn't know you were married," Emma said, looking at her from across the table. "Who's the lucky man?"

Yaz almost choked on the muffin she was eating, her assistant got up and handed her a bottle of water.

"I'm sure you don't know him, Emma," replied Yaz, with a tissue in front of her mouth.

"So, how long have you been married?" Emma said, digging deeper into her business.

"Just over a year now."

"Oh, that's right, you took almost a year off last year; medical leave wasn't it?" Emma felt herself getting caught up. "Well, congratulations, I look forward to meeting him one day, maybe you can come by the house, I'm moving in with Greg this weekend." Greg gave Emma such a look.

"Have you two lovebirds decided to tie the knot?" asked Conner, looking at Greg.

"Why don't you answer him, Greg?" said Emma in a brash tone.

"Well, as Emma and I discussed this past weekend, I wanted her to enjoy life first, marriage is a big step."

"Is that the only reason, Greg?" Emma said, staring at him with knitted brows.

"No, that's not the reason," said Yaz, pushing her chair back and standing up.

"What is going on here?" said Conner, looking at Yaz then at Emma and Greg.

"We're married."

"Who's married?" said Conner.

"Greg and I," said Yaz.

"When did this happen, Greg, and why am I hearing it like this?" said Conner, disappointment showing in his voice. "We'll talk in my office, but for now I want to celebrate, that's the reason for this breakfast meeting, a celebration, not a confession gathering."

Emma felt responsible for spoiling her own special breakfast. Everyone ate their food and slowly, one by one, left the conference room. Conner, Greg, Yaz, Emma and KJ were left seated around the table.

"I apologize for the mess," said Emma, looking around the table.

Yaz looked at her with tears in her eyes.

"I didn't want you to find out like this, Emma, you've been nothing but good to me. When I told you I was going on medical leave last year, you were so sympathetic and understanding. I decided to take the time off because I was pregnant with Greg's child. It happened the night you refused to move into the house with him, he came to my place, we talked and one thing led to another. Two months later when I told him I was pregnant, he said the right thing to do was to get married, so we tied the knot at my parents' home, before I started showing. I asked him if he was still in love with you, he never answered. Jayden, our son, was born seven months later with a rare blood disease; he lives with my parents and has to have 24-hour care. We celebrated his first birthday last week. Doctors are amazed he's lived this long."

"So, all the meetings out of town with phantom clients were visits to see Jayden, Greg?" Emma asked.

Greg replied looking down at the table.

"Yes."

"Well, whatever your motives were for keeping this relationship of lies alive, you can put them to sleep, Greg, and don't ever wake them up, which goes for you too, Yaz. We have a great working team here, let's not let our personal issues disrupt our production," said Emma sincerely.

"I'll drink to that," said Conner. "Well said."

Emma pushed her chair back, stood up and left the conference room with KJ behind her.

Eleven

"Greg, I thought you were over that," Emma said sadly, stirring up old feelings inside. "It's been five years since I was promoted and I have been one heck of a vice president, everyone has complimented me except you, what is it, Greg? You think you still love me or something, remember *you* married in secret, Greg, not me." Emma started walking out of the building. "Goodnight, Greg, as always, good job in the meeting," she said with genuine feeling, still walking toward the exit doors.

"Emma, wait," Greg called. "I'm sorry; I didn't mean to be sarcastic. Several times I wanted to come to your office and just sit and talk, like we did when you first came on board, remember...? We had a good thing going." Greg stared into Emma eyes, not knowing what to say next. "You are so beautiful, Emma, God, I was a fool," he said, feeling the hurt inside.

"Goodnight, Greg," she said, and walked through the doors, leaving Greg in the lobby of the building.

Emma drove by KJ's condo to see if she was all right. The place was in darkness, so she went to her former neighborhood hoping to find her there, but there was no sign of her. Emma was extremely worried about KJ. She drove back to her condo, parked the car and went up to her building. She knocked on the door. There was no answer the first time, so she knocked again, this time calling her name.

"KJ, open the door, it's me, Emma."

Emma tried again. This time she heard the security chain being removed from the door.

"Come in and stop yelling," KJ said as she opened the door.

"Why are you sitting here in the dark?" asked Emma.

"Thinking," KJ replied.

"Thinking about what?" Emma asked, knowing only too well it was about her releasing her past that morning.

"Emma, don't act as though my performance, if you want to call it that, was professional this morning. I said more than I should have, but somehow, now, I feel free, I feel as though my boys are resting now... I came home and sat on the sofa, I tried to reach for the light switch, but couldn't, my body was numb. In the reflection of the mirror on the wall, I saw three small bright lights and I knew it was my boys telling me it's over, now I can move on with my life, they're all right, Emm," KJ said, with tears in her eyes. "Then a sudden peace came over me. I laid down on the sofa, closed my eyes and rested... Emm, I feel like a brand new person."

Emma and KJ hugged and started laughing and crying at the same time.

"It's good to have you back, KJ, but I will not have you

missing anymore meetings," Emma said jokingly, as her boss.

"I'm sorry, how was the new line?" KJ asked, wiping her eyes.

"Fantastic... would you believe, Greg still has the hots for me."

"Get out of here," KJ responded, laughing and kicking up her heels. "I *knew* it! I see him pacing up and down the hallway passing your office maybe three or four times a day. He'll occasionally look in and give me a smile then continue, but you know Yaz is never too far away. Why did you keep them working so close to you on the same floor?"

"Because I want them to know, if they want to stop seeing my face, *they* need to make the move... out the door; no one plays with Emma Trent and walks away unscarred. I don't hate, envy or dislike, I will scar you with kindness."

"You have matured so much, I can't believe you'll be thirty tomorrow, where has the time flown to?" said KJ. "By the way, I overheard Pam, the results came back from Jayden's blood test and it looks like he's going to be okay. The treatment has been working better than the doctors expected."

"That's great news," Emma replied.

"Looks like he'll be celebrating his sixth birthday after all. I know that's a burden lifted from Yaz,"

"Yeah, I'll call her tomorrow."

"Wait until she comes to you, Emm, it's better that way."

"You're right. Anyway, I'm glad you're feeling and looking much better, and I'm looking forward to having you for dinner at my home with Aunt Lou tomorrow night in celebration of my big '3 0'."

"I'm sorry, Emm, I have to sit this one out. I promised Skye we would do the mother-daughter thing, you know."

"No, I don't know, but you have fun, I'm just glad to see you smiling again."

KJ walked Emma to the door. She felt a sense of relief knowing that she could return to work on Monday without having to explain anything.

Emma drove home, playing her music with a good feeling inside.

"Aunt Lou, I'm home," yelled Emma.

"I'm in the den," Aunt Lou replied.

Emma removed her jacket and flung it over the floral sofa in the hallway. She entered the den, walked toward Aunt Lou and gave her a kiss on the cheek.

"How was the office today?" Aunt Lou asked.

"I've had better days," replied Emma, fixing herself a drink.

"I made some baked chicken with steamed veg, hope you're hungry."

"Not really, but I'll eat a little," Emma said.

They sat at the dining table, said grace and began to eat. All of a sudden Emma said she was full.

"You barely ate a thing," said Aunt Lou.

"I know, I just have no appetite."

"Is something bothering you, Emma?" Aunt Lou asked, rather worried.

"Well, this has been bothering me for some time, almost ten years to be exact."

Aunt Lou put her knife and folk down, pushed her chair back, left the dining table and walked toward the sitting room.

"Did I say something to interrupt your dinner, Aunt Lou?" Emma said, still sitting at the table.

"No, I'm full; I need a drink to wash the food down."

"Aunt Lou, the lemonade is on the table."

"I think I'm going to need something a little stronger than lemonade."

"Why?"

"Because I think you have a lot on your mind to which you need answers."

"How would you know that, Aunt Lou?"

"Call it old wives' intuition."

Emma followed Aunt Lou into the sitting room.

"Now, tell me what's wrong," said Aunt Lou.

"How do I begin?" said Emma, standing at the bay window.

"Aunt Lou, have you ever seen someone you thought you knew,

but had never met?"

"Talk sense, Emma," said Aunt Lou, taking a sip of her drink.

"There's a lady who has been sitting on the bench at work every day for the past ten years since I've been working at MB. She's not dirty or anything, on the contrary, she's so elegant."

Emma's eyes were so bright talking about the lady, her expression was animated and she had a smile on her face. Aunt Lou laughed as she took another sip of wine.

"Why are you laughing at me, Aunt Lou?" Emma asked, turning to look at her aunt.

"I'm not laughing at you, but, you lost your appetite over a homeless woman on a park bench, what nonsense, Emma," said Aunt Lou, still chuckling.

"No, it's not that, it's the feeling that's going on inside," said Emma.

"Inside what, girl, have you lost your mind? What do you know about inside? Well, maybe you should, your mother…"

Aunt Lou paused, put her right hand over her mouth and looked at Emma with wide open eyes.

"My mother what? Please continue," Emma said, shocked that she had even mentioned her.

"No Emma, it's nothing," Aunt Lou said, looking down at the drink she had in her hand, avoiding eye contact.

"Please, Aunty, tell me, what about my mother?"

Emma walked toward her and placed her hand on her shoulder - she pulled away.

"How old are you, Emma?"

"I'm thirty tomorrow, you know that, please don't try and change the subject, Aunt Lou, please... tell me about my mother."

"Well, I guess you're old enough," she mumbled.

She walked toward the bar, poured herself another glass of wine and returned to the big, green, plaid overstuffed sofa.

"Come sit, sit right here beside me," Aunt Lou said, patting the sofa beside her.

"Your mother, my little sister," Aunt Lou began, "was a very beautiful woman."

"*Was*, Aunty?" Emma interrupted.

She gave Emma a look then continued.

"She was tall with a fair porcelain complexion, although she was black. With her straight, long honey-blonde hair and hazel eyes, she had a smile that drove men crazy."

Aunt Lou stared into space and continued. Emma could see from her expression there was a lot of pain.

"My husband's name is McIntosh Nigel Trent, everyone called him, Mint-"

"*Is*, you're still married," interrupted Emma.

Aunt Lou ignored Emma and continued talking.

"He was my first love. I was thirty years old when we married. Emmalette was twenty."

"Who is Emmalette?" Emma said, never having heard that name mentioned before.

"Your mother, Emma, that was her name, everyone called her Miss Emmalette, they said she was so beautiful she belonged with princesses."

"Aunty, why do you keep referring to her in the past tense, is she dead?"

"No." Aunt Lou looked at Emma, put her hand on her thigh and shook her head. "No, she isn't," she said very quietly. "Please pour me another drink, Emm, something strong this time."

"Don't you think you've had enough, Aunt Lou?"

"No, if I had I wouldn't ask you to pour me another one, now would I?" said Aunt Lou sarcastically. "My wedding night should have been the happiest day of my life," she continued. "Instead, it was my worse nightmare. Mint got drunk and staggered upstairs. Your mother had just taken a shower. She was never a party person, never drank, never smoked, she was almost perfect. She was in her room and Mint wandered in. He forced himself on her, but I didn't want to believe it at the time, I couldn't hear her screaming because the music was so loud.

I wondered where Mint had got to, so I went looking for him.

I went upstairs and could hear groans coming from your mother's room. I saw them in bed, her naked body pressed against his, I'll never forget the look on her face; she was so scared. I called Gracie and May, who took her into the bathroom and cleaned her up, hoping none of the guests had seen or heard anything. Two months later she found out she was pregnant - she was twenty, Mint was forty. We couldn't tell anyone, so Gracie and May decided to move out to the country and take Emmalette with them until the baby was born, we didn't want anyone asking questions. Although she was old enough to have a child, the embarrassment of not being married or even in a relationship would have tarnished the family name, so we decided I would take her to London with me. We stayed with relatives until you were born then came back to the states I couldn't bear to look at Emmalette, but even as her stomach grew, I envied her. When we came back home I asked her to leave this house and never return - she did. I never once wondered where she was, I never enquired whether she was dead or alive; all I cared about was raising you as my own. A few years later I was walking on the avenue and came across a little boutique with fine lace and linen in the window, Ms. Rose was the name of the boutique."

Aunt Lou looked at Emma as if to say, 'yes, I knew her'.

"I went in and browsed around. A young well-dressed lady

came and asked me if I needed help. When I turned around it was Emmalette, more beautiful than the last time I had seen her. I pretended I didn't know her. I could see all she wanted to do was hug me as she looked down at you standing beside me with tears in her eyes. I held your hand so tightly and walked out of the boutique. She watched from the window until we were out of sight.

I did frequent Ms. Rose's boutique, because there was no doubt she carried the finest lace, but unbeknownst to me, Emmalette was the designer of the garments, wedding gowns, you name it, she designed it. She had always been good at drawing ever since she was little.

One day I went to see Ms. Rose. I wanted her to make me a pale pink lace dress with pearlette drops on the neck and sleeves. I knew it had to be designed, I just wanted to see Emmalette again, but when I went there, Ms. Rose told me she had left to start her own business. I asked where, but she said she didn't know. I didn't believe her, but I never questioned it and neither did I visit Ms. Rose's boutique again.

While you were in high school, I started experiencing financial problems. Being still married to Mint, I started asking questions as to his whereabouts. I never received a straight answer from anyone, until on your sixteenth birthday when Gracie mentioned she had seen Mint and that he was CEO of the company for which he was working. It turned out he owned the company MINT Architects and Construction. I looked him up, and told him about you. He said he knew. I asked him how and he said Emmalette had contacted him a few years earlier with a proposal to build her the finest office building downtown and finance her own design company until it made a profit. He would own one per cent of the company for life. He agreed.

Mint sent a cheque every month to cover the bills and expenses; he paid for your four-year college degree. Emmalette knew what she was doing, she has always been smart, never drank like me, in fact she never drank at all, she always complained whenever I opened a bottle. Gracie and May couldn't care less, but Emmalette... I kept in touch with Mint, and today he still lives with someone, has a family, but she knows nothing of me or you, I promised him I'd keep it that way. He gave me an address for Emmalette.

I went there one afternoon while you were in college. It is the grandest white house anyone could ever imagine. We sat and talked, we cried, but she was only interested in you. Mint told her of the college you were attending, she made visits to see you with the help of your professors, and she made it clear to them that she didn't want you to be aware of the visits. She was there the night you graduated; I promised I would not say a word."

"Where is she, Aunt Lou, I want to meet her now, can we

go?" said Emma, standing up, demanding it of her aunt.

"Wait a minute, Emma, let me finish," Aunt Lou said, now staggering her words. "Emma, you don't have a clue do you?" she said with an envious tone to her voice. "That fancy building you work in, who do you think owns it, huh? Who do you think designed it, what do you think MB Design stands for? It's *Mint Brown* Design, Mint, your father, and Brown, the family name, your mother. It wasn't coincidence you worked with Ms. Rose. She saw the resemblance in you of Emmalette. Conner, who you think is your boss, he's your uncle, Emma, that's right, Mint's brother, and he's guaranteed one percent ownership of the company. Did it ever occur to you why no one has ever met Mr. Brown? He doesn't exist, but Miss Emmalette Brown does. The woman you call 'the lady who sits on the bench every morning and every evening', Emma, is your mother."

"What did you say, Aunt Lou?" Emma said, shocked as tears filled her eyes.

"You heard me, Emma, she told me she watches you every morning as you drive up and park your car, and in the evening you sometimes wave and give her a smile. All she ever wanted to do was hold you and tell you how much she loves you, but I held her back, I threatened to sell her secret to the papers, to ruin her if she came close to you. She told me she was going to create the position of vice president for the company as soon as Conner told her you were ready. Mint knew you were cut from the same mould, he owns your biggest contract... Squares. He sent his representative, and they said you handled the meeting better than expected."

"Why have you kept this from me all these years, Aunt Lou?" Emma said angrily.

"Because I never wanted to believe she was so powerful, so rich, so wealthy. I had to be certain and get over my own jealousy," Aunt Lou said, ashamed.

"But she's your sister, Aunt Lou, why?"

"Because I still love him, Emm, I still love him after all these years. I refused to sign the divorce papers so he could marry again," Aunt Lou said with a harsh tone to her voice. "I will never release him to marry her, I said till death do us part, and that's what I mean."

"What's gotten into you, Aunt Lou? I've never seen this horrible side of you, you're too beautiful to act like this, let it go, let it go, Aunt Lou."

"One day you'll understand, Emma, when it hits you and you wake up, you'll understand."

Aunt Lou got up from the sofa and staggered toward the bar to pour herself another drink. Emma sat there with her head in her hands.

"My mother... is that elegant lady on the park bench... I

used to think she was looking at me when I looked out of the office window, but the windows are tinted, so I brushed it off. People talk about her all the time in the elevator, there are so many stories about her. She's my mother, Aunt Lou, *my mother.*" Tears began streaming down Emma's face. "*My mother,*" she repeated.

Aunt Lou staggered back to the sofa, drink in hand, continuing to talk.

"Conner assigned your office with a clear view of the car park and park benches, didn't he?" asked Aunt Lou.

Sniffing the tears back, Emma answered.

"Yes, he did."

"Notice the door between your office and Conner's is always locked, did you ever ask why?" questioned Aunt Lou.

"How would you know about my office and Conner's, Aunt Lou?" asked Emma, reaching for a tissue.

"Emmalette took me through the building one night with Conner. There's a back elevator that leads straight to her office, she's there every evening. Conner gives her a report on you every day, like he's been doing for the past ten years. Why do you think you were given so much responsibility at such a tender age, *you* are MB Design, Emma. You have made her so proud."

Aunt Lou was slurring her words more and more.

"Then why is she hiding?" asked Emma.

"Because I asked her to stay away. I told you I threatened to expose her secret."

"Why, Aunt Lou, I'm grown now, I'm thirty years old tomorrow," said Emma, walking back toward the bay window.

"When I asked Emmalette to leave this house thirty years ago, she never looked back, but she never stopped caring and loving you. She lived in the back of Ms. Rose's boutique until the day she left and approached Mint. She was never too far away, Emma, if anyone is to blame it's me. I have always been jealous of her and hated her for having the child I never could."

Aunt Lou cried and threw the glass against the wall. Emma ran toward her and held her in her arms.

"It's okay, Aunt Lou, it's okay, I know the truth now."

Twelve

Emma had such a restless night, she cried most of the time, still in disbelief from the things her aunt had told her. She climbed out of bed and went to Aunt Lou's room. She knocked on the door - there was no answer. She knocked again - still no answer. She turned the handle - the door was locked.

Emma went downstairs into the kitchen, then the den and sitting room There was no sign of Aunt Lou. She went back upstairs and took a shower, put on a pair of jeans and a tank top, and swept her hair up into a ponytail. She slipped her feet into her flip-flops at the door, grabbed her purse and car keys. She drove to the MB building; the weekend security was on duty.

"Good morning, Miss Emma," said Stan, head of security.

He had been with MB for over fifteen years. He was a good friend of Conner's; tall, slim, an older man, but well kept.

"Good morning, Stan, how are you?" Emma said, rushing for the elevator. She turned to him. "Stan, is there another elevator in the building?"

"Why would you ask that, Miss Emma?" replied Stan, reaching for his phone.

"Don't call Conner, Stan; I know everything. Aunt Lou told me last night, now, where is the entrance to the other elevator?"

Emma asked politely.

"Okay, Miss Emma, follow me."

Stan took Emma to the back of the building where few employees had access as it was mostly used for deliveries. He took out a set of keys and ran it across the security board, releasing the latch. Emma walked toward the service elevator, pressing the button.

"That's the service elevator, Miss Emma, I think you need this one."

Emma followed Stan through a set of solid black doors, for which he used another key and swiped the security pad.

"Straight ahead, Miss Emma, this looks just like the front of the building elevator area, it is the exact replica of the elevator area, only this leads to one office, she had Mint design it that way."

Stan held his head down as he pressed the elevator button. As the doors opened there were three buttons; 'G' for ground, '9' and 'PH' for penthouse.

"How long have you known, Stan?" Emma asked as they rode up in the elevator.

"From the moment I set eyes on you, I knew you were her daughter."

"So, everyone sees except me, I don't even know what she looks like," said Emma.

The elevator stopped on the ninth floor.

"Why aren't we going to the penthouse. Stan?"

"I think you'll want to see this first."

The elevator doors opened to a dark office.

"Where are the lights, Stan?"

"Stay right there, Miss Emma, I'll put the lights on for you."

When Stan put the lights on, Emma stood there in amazement. The windows were covered in red velvet curtains, the floor was baby pink marble, the furniture pale pink glass. Emma stood there numb, scared to move, her eyes wandering around the room. There was a large portrait at the far end of the office. Emma walked toward it, she had never seen such beauty.

"Is this her, Stan?"

"Can't you see yourself?"

"No, she is more beautiful than I imagined, now I know why Aunt Lou was so jealous. When was this taken?"

"I'm not sure, Miss Emma."

"Is she still this beautiful, Stan?"

"Even more."

"Were you in love with her too, Stan?"

Emma turned to see his expression.

"Oh, no, Miss Emma, it was never like that with Miss Emmalette and me, or anyone for that matter, she was all about work. She's very soft spoken, she's never had a bad word to say about anyone or spoken harshly to anyone in all the years I've known her. She and Mint built this empire, that picture next to the portrait..."

"Yes, I was going to ask who they were."

"That's Mint and Emmalette breaking ground. Even with a shovel in her hand and wearing jeans, she still looks elegant. She designed every office and chose the same furniture for each office, and she never liked confusion."

Emma wandered around the office, she sat in her pink leather chair, leaned back and closed her eyes, and she could feel the tears just rolling down.

"Would you like me to leave, Miss Emma?"

"Please, Stan, can I have a few moments alone?"

"Just call the front desk when you're ready, Miss Emma."

"Stan, before you go, how do I get to the penthouse?"

"I'll send the elevator up for you, but you'll need this key."

Stan took the security key from around his neck and handed it to Emma.

"What about you getting out?"

"Emma, I'm head of security and have been for over fifteen years, don't worry about me, you take your time, get to know your mother, Miss Emma, I'll be downstairs."

"Thank you, Stan."

The elevator doors closed. Emma took off her flip-flops and

wandered through the office, going through drawers and cabinets, finding different things belonging to her mother. She went to a filing cabinet and opened it; there were files upon files with her name on them. She started reading. They were contracts she had signed, which Conner approved, however, now she saw they were also approved by Emmalette Brown. Emma didn't know what to think, she had mixed feelings. She continued looking around the office and stumbled upon some photos of herself while she was growing up, one for every birthday, but how, if Aunt Lou said she never knew where she was? Emma thought something wasn't right.

Emma continued to explore, opening draws, lifting papers and opening boxes, but found nothing but legitimate business contracts, proposals and legal documents.

She pressed the elevator button to go up to the penthouse. When it arrived she stepped in, swiped the key and pressed 'PH' for penthouse. The elevator doors opened and the first thing she saw was a photo of herself. The wall was full of photos of her at fashion shows and the launch of 'Elegant', her clothing line. Emma walked toward the pictures and touched them.

"I remember this, and this… how, how did she do this?" she said quietly.

She continued to the other room. There was a picture of her and KJ, again at the launch of 'Elegant'. She stood in front of the picture and took a closer look, there she was in the background - her mother

"How could I have missed her?" Emma said aloud.

"I never left you, Emma."

Emma jumped at the sound of the voice.

"Why are you standing in the shadows?" Emma asked nervously.

"I didn't want to scare you," the voice said, so softly.

"Please walk toward me, so I can see you."

As she walked toward Emma, the tall, slender most-striking beauty with flowing hair emerged into the light, as she got closer, her porcelain complexion, flawless. She stopped face to face in front of Emma, took her hand and wiped the tears falling from her daughter's face, she put her arms around her and cried.

"I have waited thirty years to do this, and it's just as I imagined, the love I feel for you has never changed over the years, never. I followed every move I could with you and wanted to leave a legacy for you in case I never got to know you."

Emma cried so hard and held her mother so tight she could not control the tears. They embraced for a while. Emma used the back of her hand to wipe her face. Her mother gently moved her hand, took both her hands and wiped the tears away, smiling at her.

"You are as beautiful in person as you are in the portrait," said Emma, staring at her mother.

"I look at me and I see every bit of you, Emma."

"How did you know I was here?" Emma asked.

"Lou called me this morning and told me everything about last night, what timing, on the eve of your thirtieth birthday."

"You remember my birthday?"

"I gave birth to you, remember."

Emmalette held Emma's hand and led her to the large white sofa, asking her to sit.

"When Lou called me this morning, I knew you would come here. She mentioned the back elevator, that's what made me know for sure you'd be here, so I got here before you did. Stan also called to let me know you were in the building."

"Why the secrecy?"

"I wanted you to work and earn whatever it was you were going for. Had you known you were wealthy, would you have worked as hard? That is something we'll never know. You have amazed me with every contract, proposal, fashion show and ultimately your own clothing line, 'Elegant'. You surely are a Trent Brown."

They both laughed.

"What do I call you?"

"My name is Emmalette, I am your mother, you are a grown woman, Emma, and you make the choice."

She looked at Emma and smiled. Emma took her hand and placed it between hers.

"You're my mother. I thought I'd be cold toward you, or something, but I don't feel that way, I feel as though I've just found my best friend." She leaned forward and hugged her mother again. "Thank you for everything, Mom, for making me the strong woman I am today."

"You have Lou to thank for that."

"She left so early this morning I didn't get a chance to see her," Emma replied.

"I know, she's here with me, Grace and May are on their way, and you can come out now, Lou," Emmalette said, so gracefully.

Emma got up from the sofa and walked toward her Aunt Lou with extended arms.

"You silly old woman, you," Emma said, with tears in her eyes.

"Silly, maybe, old, *never!*" Aunt Lou said, smiling. "I'm sorry, Emm, for telling you like I did, I am so embarrassed," she continued, holding her head down.

"Keep your head up, Lou, never let it hang. If you hadn't raised Emma, I may not have what I have today... Thank you for giving me the strength and, for what it's worth, I have never stopped loving you, and I truly never meant to cause you any pain." Emmalette rose from the chair, walked toward Emma and Lou and gave them both a hug.

"I had a lot of time to think last night, and I've decided to give Mint the divorce he's been wanting for so many years. I also called him this morning and asked him to meet me here; I need to end this once and for all."

Just then the phone rang; it was Stan, letting them know Mint was on his way up.

"Are you ready for this, Emma?"

"Yes, I am."

Emma stood strong between her mother and Aunt, and waited for the elevator door to open. As it stopped, her mother took hold of her hand and looked at her. A tall well-built man emerged from the elevator, salt and pepper hair, milk chocolate complexion. He was wearing shades. He wore a navy blue, short-sleeved linen suit, with navy and cream shoes.

"Hello, Lou, Emmalette, and you must be Emma," he said with a baritone voice.

Emma let go of her mother's hand and walked toward her father. She stood in front of him and smiled. He removed his shades.

"Hello to you, too…" she paused, "*Dad.*"

He looked at her with tear-filled eyes. He put his hand to his face and wiped his eyes.

"What is this coming from my eyes?"

"Tears," Emma said.

"Tears? Men don't cry," he said, jokingly.

"Real ones do," Emma answered back.

"I guess I'm a real man then."

Mint grabbed Emma and held her close.

"I'm sorry, Emma, for all the trouble I caused with your family, it wasn't my plan, I was foolish, drunk and had no respect for your mother or aunt. Since that night I've never touched another drop of alcohol and have no intention to ever again."

Emma stepped back to take a look at her father.

"I think Aunt Lou wants to talk to you; Mom and I will be in the other room."

Emma walked back toward her mother and Aunt Lou, holding her father's hand, leading him to the sofa.

"You did a wonderful job, Lou, thank you, thank you for many things," Mint said earnestly.

"I believe you, Mint, I need to clean my slate, and I am ready to sign the divorce papers whenever you have them ready."

"Are you serious, Lou, what's the catch?"

"There is no catch. This wonderful daughter of yours has opened many eyes, including mine. I need you to be happy, thirty years is more than enough punishment for anyone."

Aunt Lou smiled at Mint, he reached out, pulled her toward him and gave her a hug.

"I'm truly sorry, Lou, I mean that from the bottom of my heart."

"I know you do."

She gave him a kiss on the cheek then called for Emma and Emmalette to come out now.

"Is everything all right now?" Emma said, looking at her mother, father and Aunt Lou.

They all laughed, hugged and said:

"Yes."

"This has been the best birthday gift any woman could ever ask for."

"Talking about gifts, this is for you."

Emmalette handed her daughter a beautifully wrapped pink box."

"Can I open it now?" Emma asked excitedly as she tore the paper from the box. "A key for what?"

"Take a look outside."

"I see nothing but cranes, are they cleaning the windows again?" Emma asked, still looking out of the window.

"No, take another look," Mint said.

"I don't understand," Emma said, confused.

"Maybe if we go downstairs, we'll see it better."

All three entered the elevator, rode down to the ground floor and walked outside the building.

"Now look up," said Emmalette, looking at her daughter with so much pride.

Emma looked up and reached for both her parents' hands.

"Thank you... the key to the world."

"This is your world now, Emma, it's no longer MB Design it's now, 'Elegant'."

"You have earned it, from us to you, happy birthday, 'Elegant' Emma Trent."

Printed in the United States
by Baker & Taylor Publisher Services